Stunt = to attrack atension

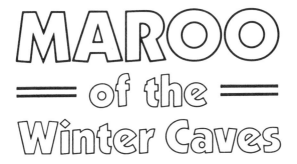

MAROO
of the
Winter Caves

Ann Turnbull

CLARION BOOKS
NEW YORK

To Tim

Clarion Books
a Houghton Mifflin Company imprint
215 Park Avenue South, New York, NY 10003
Copyright © 1984 by Ann Turnbull

For information about permission to reproduce
selections from this book,write to
Permissions, Houghton Mifflin Company,
215 Park Avenue South, New York, NY 10003.

For information about this and other Houghton Mifflin
trade and reference books and multimedia products, visit
The Bookstore at Houghton Mifflin on the
World Wide Web at (http://www.hmco.com/trade/).

Printed in the U.S.A.

Library of Congress Cataloging in Publication Data
Turnbull, Ann.
Maroo of the winter caves.
Summary: Maroo, a girl of the late Ice Age, must take charge
after her father is killed, and lead her little brother, mother and
newborn baby, and aged grandmother to the safety of the
winter camp before the first blizzards strike.
[1. Man, Prehistoric—Fiction] I. Title.
PZ7.T8493Mar 1984 [Fic] 84-4327
ISBN 0-89919-304-8   PA ISBN 0-395-54795-4

QUM   20 19 18 17 16 15 14 13 12

Contents

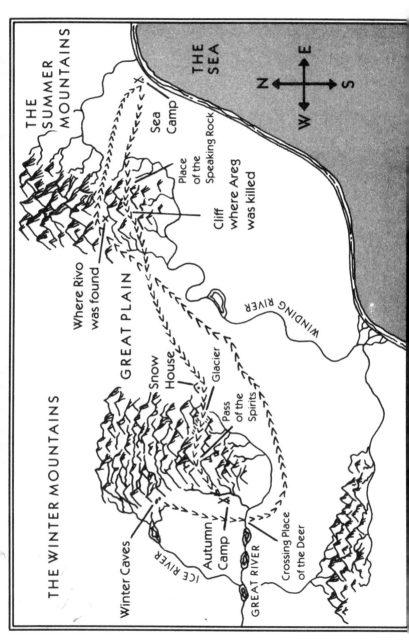

Tim Nicol

Author's Note

THIS STORY IS SET at the end of the last Ice Age in Europe. The location is based on maps of Stone Age sites in the south of France, in the Massif Central and the Maritime Alps, and the sea is the Mediterranean. However, the coastline has changed considerably since then, and the climate and geography are completely different. The people were semi-nomadic hunters. They hunted mainly reindeer and followed the deer on their long seasonal migrations. They are the people described as the Madeleine people by archaeologists.

=1=
The Thaw

MAROO WOKE HUNGRY. She lay for a moment with her eyes shut, imagining biting into tough, hot meat, savoring the charred, smoke-tasting outer part and then the salty blood within. There had been no meat for a long time, but today the hunters should return. They had left yesterday on the track of a herd of bison. Usually they came back by nightfall, but sometimes if they had hunted all day without luck, they would make camp and try again the next morning.

She opened her eyes. It was still dark in the cave, but she could see fur-wrapped shapes stirring: her mother, brother, and sister.

Nimai, the little sister, sat up and put her thumb in her mouth. Maroo reached to a niche in the cave wall and took out two dried roots. She gave one to Nimai and put one in her own mouth. The root was tough and tasteless, but it stilled the hunger pains.

Maroo found her boots and pulled them on. They were made of soft leather, trimmed with white fox fur.

She tucked her deerskin trousers inside them and tied them in place with leather thongs.

The place where they slept was a recess in the wall of the inner cave. Skins were piled across the entrance to keep out drafts. There were recesses and sleeping platforms all around. Hardly any floor space was left in the small cave. More people lived here than Maroo could count using all her fingers twice.

"Maroo!"

Nimai had followed her out, thumb in mouth and boots untied. Maroo tied the boots and said, "We'll go outside and look for herbs."

They turned the corner into the outer cave. At once the air felt cold. A misty gray dawn showed in the cave mouth. Old Mother was squatting there, scraping away the ash from last night's fire. Maroo watched as Old Mother put her face close to the blackened wood in the hearth-place and blew gently. Her warm breath woke the sleeping fire; a thread of scarlet quivered in one of the pieces, then vanished. Old Mother blew again. Smoke rose from the embers, then little yellow flames sprang from the wood and joined to make bigger flames. The children squatted beside their grandmother. Old Mother brought small pieces of the precious wood from her store and fed the hungry flames. They grew fat and red, and their warmth beat upon the girls' faces.

The fire was built inside a circle of boulders surrounded on three sides by large, flat stones where people could sit. The flames were leaping up brightly now, and points of fire shone in Old Mother's dark eyes. There was a bone dish beside the fire full of small, smooth, round stones. The old woman dropped them gently into the heart of the fire. When they were hot she would put them into a bowl of water to make warm drinks.

Old Mother patted Maroo's hand. "Find something good to drink."

Maroo nodded. She knew her grandmother liked hot water flavored with herbs. "Will the hunters come home today, Old Mother?" she asked. "Will we have meat?"

"Will the snow melt? Will the grass grow?" Old Mother pretended despair at the questions. "You should ask the spirits such things, not an old woman." She chuckled. "They will come today. I feel it, here" — she struck her chest — "and we shall have full bellies tonight, eh, little one?" She patted Nimai's stomach. Nimai squirmed and giggled.

"Be off with you," said Old Mother, "and find me some good herbs."

Outside the cave the land sloped gently down a pebbly hillside scattered with stunted trees toward the lake. The spring thaw had made the scree slippery; the pebbles rolled under their feet as they started down, and Nimai would not go alone but clung timidly to Maroo's hand. The path was running with water, and the sound of water was all around, from the dripping, close by, of snow from the cave roof where the fire was melting it, to the distant roar of countless streams. From far away on the river, beyond the lake, farther than the children could see, came the faint crashing of ice floes.

They stopped at the bottom of the slope.

"Hear the river," said Nimai.

Maroo imagined the unseen river, liberated after the long winter, rushing and tumbling down from the mountains, carrying rocks, bones, broken trees, drowned animals, and smashed-up ice to the sea. The sea was harder to imagine, for she had never seen it, though some of her kinsmen had, and had brought back the shells that decorated her jacket. If only . . . Maroo thought of the coming summer, and wished: if only this summer we could go to the sea. She had wished it before, but either they had never gotten so far or they had taken a different way, up into the mountains. Perhaps this year they would go.

Maroo loved the summer with its uncertainty about where they would be from one day to the next. All winter they had scarcely left the cave, hemmed in by blizzards that blew for days on end, and a cold so intense that an unprotected finger or toe could freeze and drop off. But soon—perhaps in a few days' time if the hunters were lucky—they would leave the caves and spend the summer wandering, until the cold weather and the migrations of the reindeer brought them back to the autumn hunting grounds.

Maroo did a little dance of excited anticipation. Nimai laughed and jumped about.

"We'll go soon," said Maroo. "We'll follow the deer!"

Nimai grinned. "Fish!" she said. "Honey!"

Nimai was old enough to remember the pleasures of last summer.

Maroo led Nimai down to the shore of the lake where green shoots were showing through the melting snow. They began to search for berries and plants with thick roots that could be eaten. They found a patch of the shrub they called "drops of blood" with its little sour red berries, and soon filled a small basket. Nimai kept eating the berries, and Maroo scolded her, though she furtively ate a few herself. Nearby they found a plant with strongly scented leaves. Maroo squatted down to gather a handful, glad that she could please Old Mother. Nimai wandered to the water's edge.

"Come away!" Maroo shouted.

"See my spirit!" said Nimai.

Maroo came to look. The ice that had covered the lake all winter was melting, revealing large stretches of still gray water. Nimai's small, smiling spirit form was looking up at her from the lake. The spirit of Maroo came up and stood beside it. The gently moving shape had a round face framed by brown wolverine fur and two dark plaits of hair hanging down on its chest. She put up a hand to stroke the fur, and the spirit copied her.

A stone hit the water with force and smashed the image. Both girls jumped in fright.

Maroo sprang round. "Otak!"

Her younger brother stood grinning at her, the sling loose in his hand. Maroo jumped on him and punched him. "You drove my spirit away!"

But she was laughing; she knew it would come back. They fought playfully. Nimai knelt by the water, watching the spreading rings.

Maroo and Otak began quarreling over the berries.

"Don't you eat those!" she said sharply. "Stay here and watch Nimai while I take the basket to Old Mother."

"That's girl's work —" Otak began.

But Maroo ignored him and ran back to the cave. When she returned, Otak was skimming a flat stone across the water. It jumped twice, to Nimai's delight.

"Again!" the little girl said.

She darted about, fetching Otak stones, always the wrong shape. Maroo found him a better one. He was poised for a throw when Nimai began to shout:

"Men! Hunters!"

Otak dropped the stone and they all stared where she was pointing. Far away, along the lake shore, Maroo saw a movement. Could it be the hunters, or was it animals? Nimai was already jumping up and down.

The next moment Maroo knew. "Yes!" she exclaimed. "They're coming!"

Nimai began to scream with excitement.

Otak turned toward the cave and leaped high in the air, waving his arms and shouting. A distant voice answered him.

"Quick! Run!" Otak said to Maroo. "We'll be first!"

=2=
The Spring Killing

OTAK AND MAROO were off like spring hares. Behind them they heard the furious cries of their little sister, but neither would stop to wait. Women were coming down to the lakeside, and they would comfort Nimai.

The hunters approached steadily. Otak and Maroo made out the shape of a large animal tied by its feet and hanging between two poles. Four men carried the poles. The leaders were Tevo and their own father, Areg.

They ran faster, delighted to be first to greet the hunters. When they reached them, they stood, breathless, unable to speak.

Tevo said modestly, "We have not had much luck. Just this small animal."

Otak and Maroo smiled. They knew that such modesty was feigned, merely the politeness expected of hunters who have made a magnificent kill. Their father made a joke of it, pretending to stagger under the weight of the beast. The children shouted with laughter, but Tevo gave Areg a disapproving look.

Otak signaled to the distant group of women who

8

had gathered by the lakeside. He put his hands to his forehead, curving them like horns. The women knew this meant a bison. They began to move back up the slope toward the cave.

Behind Tevo and Areg came the other hunters. Areg's brother, Vorka, carried the spears. Otak chattered to Vorka, and the young man told him about the hunt as they walked back to the cave.

Everyone was waiting at the cave mouth. The women helped to lower the great animal onto the flat ground outside the cave, and immediately began flaying it with sharp stone knives. Blood was collected in a bowl made from a deer's skull, and passed around for the hunters to drink. Old Mother, meanwhile, had made the fire hot and was giving drinks of herb-flavored water to the women and children.

One of the elders, Keriatek, brought out a small drum and began to tap a rhythm. The women sang as they worked. Maroo and an older girl were given stone scrapers and set to cleaning every scrap of flesh from the flayed skin. It was hard work, but they joined in the singing and thought of the feast to come. The liver and other soft parts were cut out and eaten raw, but the children had none: the hunters came first.

Before long the carcass was jointed, and chunks of meat were stuck on sticks and roasting over the fire. Fat splashed, sizzling, into the flames. Maroo, still scraping at the hide, felt limp with hunger.

At last enough meat was cooked for the feast to begin. Old Mother called everyone to stop working and come to eat. Maroo was handed a meaty bone. It was so hot she almost dropped it. But she was too hungry to care about getting burned, and began tearing at the hot flesh with her teeth.

The feast lasted all day. They did not eat all the time, but stopped to talk and sing and tell stories. The hunters were tired and stretched, yawning, by the fire, but Nimai made sure her father did not fall asleep. She climbed onto his knees and giggled as he tossed her about and fed her tidbits. Vorka smiled quietly at Areg's games; he lived in his elder brother's shadow.

Soon Vorka slipped away to the back of the cave and came back with Areg's drum. He offered it to his brother, who was a renowned drummer. Nimai squealed as Areg swung her down and took the drum. He began to experiment with a rhythm. The small drum was made of hide stretched over bone and decorated with fox-fur pompoms on thongs that spun outward as Areg tossed and caught the drum and tapped a complex rhythm. Everyone began to clap and sing.

Many hours later they were still eating. The drum and voices were silent; the fire had dimmed to a warm glow. All around the outer cave people lay on the stone hearth seats or on skins on the floor. The hunters had fallen asleep. Nimai, lolling on her mother, was sucking her thumb and twisting a greasy finger in her hair. Maroo curled up on the floor and soon fell asleep.

She woke to the chattering of women as they cleared

away the bones from the feast. It was morning. Old Mother was heating her stones in the fire and pinning up her hair with carved bone pins.

Maroo yawned and sat up.

Old Mother said, "Today we leave for the summer hunting."

Maroo scrambled eagerly to her feet. Her first thought was for her treasures. She ran into the inner cave and reached up to a hole in the rock. The wall next to the hole was marked with a scratched outline of a ptarmigan, the bird she was named for. She pulled out necklaces, a skin bag full of shells and bone beads, a reed whistle. She put all the necklaces over her head. Already hanging from her belt was a skin bag containing stone knives: a sharp one for cutting, a flaying knife, a scraper, and one for boring holes. In another bag she carried bone needles and sinews for sewing and, most important of all, a bow-drill for fire-making.

The inner cave was almost empty. It looked strange with all the fur bedding gone. The tribe had few possessions and could break camp quickly, even after the long cold. The men would carry the sledges and snowshoes only for three days; then they would leave them, hidden in a cleft of rock, at the Crossing Place of the Deer on the Great River, to await the people's return at the onset of winter.

Everyone carried something. Only the hunters would travel light, to be ready with sling or spear whenever the chance arose. The women and girls would carry babies and backpacks of furs and clothing. Strong younger women without children would carry on their backs the bundles of heavy hides for covering shelters.

Tikek, Maroo's mother, was in the sleeping place, shaking out furs. She said, "Help me roll these."

Maroo picked up a wolverine fur. It smelled musty when she shook it. "Mother!" she pleaded. "Can we go to the sea this summer?"

Tikek straightened up, tossing back her long black hair. She was expecting a baby in the summer, and already it was beginning to show. She put a hand on her belly and smiled as she said, "This one will decide what we do."

And Maroo had to be content with that.

She found her brother on the edge of a circle of men. They were drawing maps in the ash with a piece of bone and talking about the routes they might take when the tribe split up into smaller groups for the summer. Maroo peered at the pattern of lines. She could recognize the home cave, and the lake on the Ice River, and south of that the Great River with the shallow crossing place where the deer converged in autumn.

Areg was pointing to the trail that curved in a huge arc around the foothills of the White Mountain to reach the plain on the far side. A much shorter trail crossed the White Mountain itself, but no one had used it for many years. There were cave lions there, and a dangerous glacier, but it was the spirits that the tribe feared most. Old Mother, who had climbed the trail long ago, believed that the mountain spirits were unfriendly to people, and Tikek said that she never felt easy until they were well past the mountain and out on the open plain.

Otak whispered to Maroo, "I wish we could take the White Mountain trail. I want to see a cave lion."

Maroo shivered. She had never seen a cave lion, but she had seen their bones, and she knew what they were like: huge, tawny animals standing almost shoulder-high to a man, with long, cruel teeth and claws that could kill a hunter with one swipe.

"I don't want to see one," she said. And yet she knew it was not the thought of the lions that gave her that strange feeling whenever the tribe passed the White Mountain: it was the spirits. She did not know what a spirit was; she had often asked the adults about them, but no one could tell her. She sensed that the spirits were something much more to be feared than wild beasts. Yet mixed with her fear of the mountain was curiosity: why shouldn't people cross it, and what would happen to them if they did?

=3=
On the Great Plain

AREG SHADED HIS EYES against the early-morning snow dazzle on the plain and stared at the distant line of hills. "There!" he said, pointing.

Maroo squinted. Faint against the faraway gray rock she saw a dark vertical line. She knew what it was: a wooded gorge. There they would find trees for building and firewood, green food to eat, and fresh water from the hills. Such places were rare, but the people knew them all. They were long past the White Mountain now and out on the Great Plain. The plain was a vast, flat expanse, marshy in places and covered with moss and stunted trees that grew no higher than Maroo's boots. It looked empty, yet Areg had navigated it and brought them within sight of the camping place he remembered.

It took them half the morning to reach the gorge. They were a smaller group now: only the two hunters Areg and Vorka, Old Mother and her daughter, and the three children. The tribe had broken into several groups, one going up into the hills, another staying to fish by the shores of a lake, but all moving slowly northeast in the wake of the deer. Food was so abundant in summer that it was not necessary to travel in a large group. The young men were glad of the chance to lead, and everyone was glad to be away from the quarrels and closeness of the cave.

As they walked, the familiar deer smell came to them on the wind. The reindeer passed farther to the north, following their ancient trails; the ground vibrated constantly under their hundreds of hooves. Sometimes a herd of bison or mammoth would appear in the distance, and sometimes they saw rival predators: wolves, wild dogs, or a lone wolverine. Near the entrance to the gorge they found the skeleton of a horse, picked clean by scavengers.

Inside the gorge was a different world, green and rippling with bird song. Water came sparkling down from a spring in the hills above. There were willows growing by the stream, and a small grove of birch close against the steep rock face.

They all ran to the stream and drank, then sat down to rest on the rocks and share chunks of cold deer meat.

When they had eaten, the men began discussing where to build a hut. The children wanted to help, but Old Mother said, "We must find fresh food."

Maroo brightened. Green food was welcome after the long winter months of nothing but meat and stored nuts. She fetched the grass bags the women had woven during the winter. These had long handles that could be carried over the shoulders, leaving the hands free to dig and scrape. There were bone digging sticks and sharp flint cutters for each person.

Maroo handed out the bags: one each for herself and Otak, a tiny one for Nimai, and larger ones for her mother and grandmother.

The men had already begun digging the base of the hut, close under the rock overhang. This was the hardest part of the work. They grunted as they swung the sharp antler picks, but for all their efforts they were scarcely breaking the surface of the ground, which was still rock-hard under the melting snow.

Old Mother led her party deep into the wooded gorge, and the rhythmic sound of the picks gradually faded. The snow higher up the slopes was beginning to melt and run in rivulets and small streams down the sides of the hills, forming a lush marshy woodland at the bottom. They found blue flowers with long, wet green leaves. The leaves were tough, but when the plant was dug up it yielded a soft white root that was good to eat. Maroo ate several, enjoying the fresh earthy taste.

Nimai came and helped with her own little digging stick. As they jabbed their sticks into the soft earth, beetles and worms were disturbed. Nimai caught a beetle and put it into her mouth, but it was hard and bitter and she spat it out.

Maroo laughed as she tossed roots into her bag.

"Beetles are no good to eat," she said. "Find some grubs."

Maroo put up her head and sniffed the air. The gorge was full of damp woodsy smells: moss, and crushed leaves, the tang of the white roots and the crumbly earth, and mixed in with all these Maroo thought she detected a faint smell of goat.

"I smell grubs," Nimai declared confidently, and trotted off. Maroo laughed. "Grubs have no scent," she called. But a few minutes later she heard Nimai squealing, "Grubs! Grubs! Quick!"

Maroo jumped up. Nimai was poking at a piece of rotting wood with her stick and popping things into her mouth. Everyone came running. Out of the soft crumbled wood, fat white grubs were scurrying in all directions. Quick hands snatched at them. Maroo grabbed and ate the grubs as fast as she could. They were soft and juicy, with a sharp taste. Nimai laughed to see them run.

When the excitement was over, Old Mother said she had seen some bushes with sweet leaves higher up one of the sides of the gorge. They followed her out of the wet valley bottom into the more open area below the snowline.

They picked busily. Tikek, who was tired because of the coming baby, stayed with Old Mother on the lower slopes, but the children climbed higher, scrambling over rocks and finding insects under loose stones.

The goat smell was stronger here. A scatter of falling stones made them look up in time to see the rump of an ibex disappearing behind the rocks higher up.

Otak's eyes sparkled and his hand moved instinctively to his small spear. He knew he could never catch an ibex, but he could not resist chasing them. The ibex were so beautiful. Two more had appeared, their heads crowned with thick ridged horns curving back in a perfect arc. The children stared. The goats stared warily back. The children scrambled up the slope, and the ibex clattered a little higher. The children moved again, and again the ibex climbed higher.

Nimai laughed; she loved chasing things. But then the two older children, caught up in the fun of the chase, climbed swiftly up the steep hill and out of her sight, the goats leaping away ahead of them. Nimai could not follow and went back wailing to her mother.

Otak and Maroo stopped, panting, at the top of the hill. The wind hit them as they reached the summit, almost knocking them over. They crouched for shelter behind a rock. The hilltop was bare and cold, scattered with outcrops of gray rock and with large drifts of snow where the sun hadn't yet ventured. There was nothing here to put in their bags.

"Let's go back," said Maroo. "It's cold."

But Otak had heard something. He signaled to her to be quiet.

Maroo listened. Between the loud gusts of wind she

heard a high, faint whimpering, like that of an animal in pain.

The children looked at each other. Both were curious.

Maroo signaled, "Let's find it."

They crept forward. Otak held his spear at the ready.

=4=
Wild Dog

OTAK WENT FIRST, because he had the spear. He cast about for the direction of the whimpering; it was blown on the wind and hard to place, and for a long time it stopped altogether. Then they both heard it again, near at hand, coming from some rocks just ahead of them.

Maroo squinted against the bright light bouncing off the snow. Otak was a dark, moving blur; it hurt her eyes to look at him. He moved cautiously. She saw him stop and signal to her to come.

He was leaning on a low rock. They both peered over it. On the far side lay a wild she-dog, dead. Her flank was ripped open. Beside her a puppy with an injured foreleg whimpered pathetically and nuzzled at her teats. The prints of the dog pack led away from the two in their patch of blood-trampled snow.

The puppy saw the children and cringed, snarling, its yellow eyes dilated with fear, but it could not move. They saw that it would soon die, if not from cold and hunger, then from attacks by eagles or other carnivores. Maroo wondered what had happened; perhaps the mother had died defending her pup.

She crept softly toward the puppy, followed by Otak. The puppy tried to scramble away, holding up its leg, but collapsed panting. It growled fearfully.

The children whispered together.

"What killed her?"

"Maybe a bear?"

"Perhaps. But she looks as if she might have been gored."

"The puppy will die if we leave it."

"It might die anyway without its mother."

"No. It must have been weaned."

They both fell silent, thinking.

Maroo said, "Perhaps we could take it back to the camp?"

She had put the thoughts of both of them into words.

"The grownups will be angry," Otak said. "They'll tell us to drive it away."

Maroo guessed he was right. After all, what use was a dog? Dogs were rivals of people, and a sick one would take precious food. Yet she knew that people had sometimes tamed dogs. There was a man from the Blue Lake tribe who had one. She had seen it at the autumn gathering last year, wearing a leather collar and following him around as if he were its pack leader. The man took the dog with him when he went hunting. Many people thought the man crazy to give food and shelter to a dog, but Maroo had noticed how the dog loved the man and watched for him and rushed joyfully to meet him when he had been away.

Tentatively, she put out a hand to stroke the puppy. It showed its gums and snarled with yellow, pointed teeth. She dared not touch the injured leg. "I think I could bandage it," she said, "but he won't let me."

Otak rummaged in the bag hanging from his belt and brought out the leather mittens he wore in cold weather. "I could hold him," he said.

"He'll bite through those."

"Let me try."

Maroo looked in her own bag. She carried strips of soft leather for binding wounds. To clean the wound she melted some snow in her hand. "Now," she said.

Otak got behind the puppy. He put one arm around its body and held its head with the other mittened hand, leaving the forepaw dangling. The puppy struggled fiercely, and Otak nearly lost his grip. "He's strong!" he exclaimed.

"Can you hold him?"

"I think so." Otak held on, wincing as the puppy's teeth pierced his mittens, while Maroo gently cleaned the bloody wound.

She had to force herself to tend the leg; the pain was so great that the puppy's whole body jerked at every touch, and she hated the feeling that she was hurting him.

Otak was restraining the dog bravely. Quickly she

began binding the wound. When it was done she knotted another strip of hide and made a collar with a lead. She slipped the collar over the dog's head, and his eyes rolled in terror. He freed his muzzle from Otak's hand and twisted his head around, trying to bite off the strange thing.

"I wish we had food for him," said Maroo.

"There's meat at the camp."

"But will they let him eat?"

"We can't leave him now."

"No."

Maroo put on her own mittens, and they took turns carrying the fierce little creature back to the woodland. With difficulty they began climbing down the steep hillside. Maroo took the dog, winding the lead several times around her wrist and holding on grimly. Otak went down quickly on his own, and she heard his high-pitched voice describing to the others what had happened, and the disapproving lower tones of the women.

When Maroo arrived, clutching the dog, the two women were already telling Otak that he could not keep it.

Maroo talked about the man from the Blue Lake tribe, but Old Mother was not impressed. "Perhaps in the caves, in the winter, it might be possible," she conceded, "but not now, when we are on the move."

Maroo seized on that "perhaps." "He'll soon learn to run again," she said. "He could stay with us, and help us hunt, and follow us when we go back to the caves."

Old Mother sighed and shook her head. But Tikek said, "Put him down, Maroo. See if he can walk."

Maroo set the puppy down gently. He ran a little way, with the bad leg held stiffly off the ground, but soon stopped and began his high-pitched whimpering.

"The leg will mend," Tikek said. "Maroo has bandaged it well."

"And he's just a puppy," Otak agreed eagerly. "He'll be easy to tame."

Tikek squatted down and held out her hand and called softly to the dog. He stared with wild eyes but did not try to move away.

"He's hungry," Maroo said, turning pleading eyes on Old Mother.

"There is plenty of food in summer," Tikek admitted.

Maroo saw that she now had her mother on her side, and felt hopeful. Tikek was submissive, content to be led by the old woman and the men, but when she truly wanted something she usually got her way.

"Can't we try to tame him?" Maroo begged, and Otak and Nimai joined in, "Please, can we try?"

"I don't know what the men will say," Old Mother said, shaking her head. The children jumped with glee. "Take him back to the camp. Areg can decide."

Maroo was jubilant. She knew that Areg would be guided by Old Mother, and Old Mother had half-heartedly agreed. Of course, the elders might object, but the family would not come under their leadership again until the autumn, and by that time surely the dog would be tame.

When they returned to the camp, the first thing they noticed was the hut, almost finished. The men had cut willow branches, which they had set into the base, bending them over and crisscrossing them to make a low domed building. Smaller branches had been woven in and out between the main stems.

They saw the men sitting on stones by the stream. Their barbed harpoons and several large salmon lay beside them.

Otak ran to his father, exclaiming in disappointment, "I wanted to fish! Why didn't you wait for me?"

Areg mimicked Otak's sulky face. "Another time, little hunter."

Before Otak could protest, Maroo was there with the puppy. Both men jumped up.

"What's this?"

Everyone began explaining at once.

"Can we keep him?" the children begged.

Vorka looked at Areg anxiously. "He will eat a lot. And what will the elders say?"

Areg shrugged. He was trying to touch the puppy in Maroo's arms, but the sharp teeth snapped at him. Maroo could see that her father was fascinated. The puppy growled. Areg growled back. The puppy barked furiously.

"Don't!" said Maroo. "You're making him cross."

Areg laughed. "He's a fierce one!"

"Can he stay?"

"Yes," said Areg. "He can stay."

The children shouted their happiness.

"And now," said Old Mother, "we must finish the hut before we eat. It will soon be dark. Put the puppy down, Maroo, and fetch the hides."

Maroo tied the dog's lead to a tree. They all helped to stretch hides across the willow framework of the hut and tie them in place. Soon it was done. The men fetched big stones and used them to wedge the base firmly. The small round house crouched under the rock wall, too low to be battered by the wind. Old Mother lit the fire while Tikek gutted the fish and prepared vegetables.

Maroo brought water to the puppy in a bone bowl and begged a bit of raw deer meat from her mother. She chopped the meat small, and the puppy ate ravenously. The children stood around watching him. He snarled at them, his eyes widening with fear.

"Come away! You make him afraid," Old Mother said.

But the children were unable to stay far away until the fish was cooked and Tikek called them to come and eat. When they went to look at him after the meal, the puppy was asleep.

"Now leave him, and let his wound mend," said Old Mother firmly as all three crouched beside the puppy and Nimai tentatively stroked his head.

Maroo seized her advantage. "Tell us a story, Old Mother!" she begged.

The younger children immediately began to clamor for a story too, and even Areg and Vorka joined in; everyone loved a story. So, as the night deepened and the stars came up cold and bright, they huddled close together around the fire and listened.

Maroo's gaze was fixed on Old Mother's face as she began. Old Mother was very old, her skin like soft, creased leather, her cheeks collapsed inward over teeth that were worn flat from chewing hides to soften them. Only her eyes were still young, not filmy like some of the old men's, but dark, and bright as a knife. The story she told was one about the time when the gods walked the earth, after the Great Mother, Omma, had given birth to the lesser gods on the Great Ice. Last of all had come Ptarmigan, and she was the cleverest of all the gods. There were many tales of her cunning, and Old Mother told one that they had all heard many times before: how Ptarmigan outwitted Wolverine. Maroo was pleased; she loved these stories because her own name meant "Little Ptarmigan."

When the story was over, the children went to look at the puppy. It was still asleep, but its legs were twitching.

"He's chasing the Dream Hare," Old Mother said.

═5═
A New Friend

MAROO DID NOT WANT to move the puppy, so she fetched stones from under the rock overhang and built a little shelter around him to keep off the wind, and laid branches across it. In the morning, when she and Otak crawled eagerly out of the shelter to see him, the branches had blown away, but the puppy was evidently still alive; they could hear him whining and scratching at the lead.

Old Mother was tending the fire. "Your new friend is hungry," she remarked.

"I'll fetch meat," said Maroo.

"No! I want to," Otak said.

"It's a girl's job."

"You fed him last night. He's my dog too."

They were still quarreling as they went to fetch the leftover bones from the last of the deer meat. Maroo gave in and said sulkily, "I'll get clean water for him. But tomorrow I shall feed him."

When she came back from the stream, the puppy was eating and Otak was squatting nearby, watching him.

Old Mother's fire was burning well. She left it and came to squat beside them.

"He should have a name," Maroo said. "What shall we call him?"

"You will have to untie him soon," Old Mother warned. "In a few days we may leave this camp. You will have enough to carry without him. He must be untied. And he may not follow us."

"How soon will we leave?" Maroo asked anxiously.

The old woman shrugged. Such things were never planned; they depended on the availability of food and the mood of the people.

Maroo wondered how long it would take to tame the puppy; he still snarled savagely whenever she put out a hand. She realized that Old Mother thought he might not follow when they left and did not want the children to become too fond of him.

"Don't name him yet," Old Mother said. "Once you give him a name, his spirit will be in your keeping. Wait until we leave. Then untie him, and if he follows us, name him."

The camp was a good one, and they stayed more days than Maroo could count, living on fish, hares, and the green food they found in the woods. Full summer came. The bitter winds subsided; there were no more snow showers, and the last patches of snow melted away. There were flowers to pick on the hillsides: small pink azaleas and fat cushions of moss with starry white blossoms. Patches of bright yellow lichen appeared on the bare rocks, and in the damp valley bottom there was moss of a deep green color furred with tiny golden fronds.

Nobody worked hard in this season. Vorka made the children pipes and whistles out of bones, engraving pictures on them of deer's heads, plants, and fish. Areg made a new drum. Around the rim of it he tied clusters of little bones that clunked together as he beat the rhythm. They danced all one afternoon to celebrate the making of the new drum. That was the day they saw a wisp of smoke rising from behind a large rock far out on the plain.

Areg pointed to the smoke. "Sovi's fire," he said.

They knew that it must be Sovi's group. Keriatek and his sons had gone straight up into the hills, and their fire would not be visible. The next day Areg and Vorka walked across the plain to Sovi's camp, and the two groups of men went hunting together and brought back a deer.

During this time Otak and Maroo gradually made friends with the dog. One day he took meat from Otak's hand. He still backed away if they tried to pat him, but they saw that his fear was going.

They began taking him into the shelter to sleep, but they still tied him to one of the supports. Then one night Maroo brought him in but did not tie him up. He fell asleep, but in the morning his place was empty.

Maroo crawled out, her heart fluttering. Had she given him his freedom too soon?

There at the hearth-place was Old Mother, and a few yards away, wary but hopeful, sat the dog. When he saw Maroo, he got up and his tail wagged. Maroo fetched bones from the deer, and he trotted eagerly toward her.

They stayed in the gorge until the last night of the old moon. Sovi's group stayed too, in their camp on the plain. The two groups had decided to combine and go on together toward the seashore. The women had suggested this. With the bigger group, there would be five hunters, and another woman — Avni — to help Tikek when the time came for the new baby to be born.

On the last evening the children ran about excitedly. Otak pretended to be a deer, and the girls chased him with imaginary spears. The puppy barked and wagged his tail and jumped up at the girls. The adults sat talking around the fire. No one was busy; there was nothing to pack. The sun was setting behind the gorge, and the enormous sky was streaked pink and gold. Far away on the plain, water flashed, and a slight, persistent dark movement betrayed the presence of vast herds of deer.

Areg began to sing. It was a song about summer and the animals that could be hunted. The children stopped playing and gathered around. Everyone joined in the choruses and clapped the rhythm.

The rhythm was complicated, and Maroo had to concentrate to keep it right. When Areg stopped singing, they all clapped on, enjoying the intricacies of the pattern they were making. Maroo saw that Otak was dreaming as usual and clapping without thinking. Tikek had seen it too. She caught her daughter's eye and they grinned at each other; then Tikek introduced a new rhythm into the clapping. Maroo picked it up at once, but Otak stumbled, lost it, and stopped. Maroo and Tikek collapsed, laughing. Nimai joined in the laughter without knowing why.

The night cold came quickly. The clapping game broke up, and they began crawling into the hut to sleep. The sky was a deep blue now, full of stars. Sovi's smoke was no longer visible.

Maroo crawled into her place in the hut between Otak and Nimai, wrapping herself closely with the furs. Outside she heard the wind prowling around the shelter, lifting the edges of the skin covering and pushing at the frame. She shivered, with fear more than cold, and snuggled against Nimai's warm little body. The dog, lying by her feet, whimpered softly as she moved. He seemed tame now, but would he leave the gorge with them? She lay awake for some time, listening to the soft breathing of the sleeping family and thinking anxiously about the dog.

In the morning she woke and saw Old Mother silhouetted in the doorway, arranging her hair. It was a comforting sight. Nearly every morning of her life she had watched Old Mother plait her hair and coil the plaits into a cone shape on top of her head, fixing it with three bone pins: one engraved with a pattern of deer heads, one with rippling lines like water, and, Maroo's favorite, the one carved in the round to make the stretched-out body of a running deer. The pins were old, and worn smooth and yellow with use. They had been carved by Old Mother's grandfather and passed down through the family for years.

Old Mother saw Maroo watching her and smiled, sensing the girl's anxiety. "It is time to go," she said gently.

They rolled up the furs and untied the skins from the frame of the shelter. The bundles were shared out.

When they left the gorge, the frail shelter stood open to the wind; soon it would collapse. All that would mark the place would be a few bones and a charred patch where the fire had been.

The dog stood barking by the empty hearth-place. This was the moment for which Maroo had been holding herself in readiness. She was trembling as she set off along the trail and turned to whistle to the dog. The dog stiffened at the sound, and his ears pricked up. Then, without hesitating, he bounded along the trail to join her.

Maroo exclaimed joyfully, "He's coming, Old Mother! He's coming!" The children fussed over the dog, and he licked their hands and wagged his tail as he ran alongside them.

Old Mother said, "Now you must name him."

Maroo and Otak had already thought of a name.

"We will call him Rivo," Maroo said. The name meant "friend."

Old Mother approved. "It is a good name."

They turned toward the east. Spread out across the plain, a brown tide of reindeer was moving endlessly in the same direction.

=6=
The Sea

THE JOURNEY EAST to the sea took half a moon. Vorka notched the days on the bone amulet he was making. It was a flattish blade bone with a hole bored at the narrow end. Vorka threaded it on a leather strip and wore it around his neck, and whenever they stopped for a few days he would take it off and add a few more symbols of their journey: scratched outlines of a hare, a spear, and a wild dog; wavy lines for rivers; a deer's head looking backward over its shoulder.

They were crossing the lower slopes of a great mountain range, much higher than the mountains above the winter caves. Perpetual snow covered the heights. Maroo knew this range as the Summer Mountains because the deer sought out these high, cold pastures in summer. As they climbed higher, the land became more arid. Trees for firewood were scarce, but the people knew where to find the clumps of stunted birch and willow that grew in sheltered crevices.

Tikek was getting big. She wanted to reach the seashore and have the baby there, but she had to stop and rest more often now, and the other adults began to wonder if it was too far to go. Maroo liked to put her hand on her mother's belly and feel the baby kicking. "It wants to be born," she said, but Tikek said, "Not yet."

For several days they camped in the mountains at a place where clear, cold water sprang from the heart of the rock and went leaping down to the plain. There was a river nearby where the fish were so plentiful that Maroo and Otak could catch them in their hands. And although Maroo was still dressed in her furs, she also wore garlands of the white and purple saxifrage flowers that grew all over the mountain.

When they left the mountain camp, they began to climb slowly but steadily downhill every day. Sovi and Areg and Old Mother knew this trail, but to the others it was new. One morning, when an east wind was blowing, Maroo woke and was aware of a strange smell, far away still, but unlike anything she had smelled before. There was salt in it, and other scents she could not define.

Old Mother, who was heating stones in the fire, smiled as she saw Maroo examining the air. "It is the sea," she said.

A few days later, Maroo saw for the first time the thing she had smelled. They came to a gap between two hills, and, looking down, instead of the expected green plain they saw a gray expanse of water that stretched forever. Only this water was not flat and clear like a lake, but constantly moving, and dimpling with flashes of light and changing color, gray and green and violet. The distant, tantalizing smell now surrounded them, telling Maroo of salt, seaweed, fish, and all the creatures that lived in the sea.

They climbed down to the white, sandy beach, disturbing colonies of gulls that flew upward, screaming. The children had never seen sand before. They dug holes, drew lines, piled it up, and rolled in it. Rivo rushed from one to another of the children, wagging his tail. He scrabbled in the beach, sending sand flying. As they scampered about, squealing with excitement, the sea startled them by running up and then retreating with a hiss. Rivo barked at it.

Old Mother had been to this beach before. She remembered that there was a cave big enough to make a home, and sent the children off to look for it.

The children ran up and down the long beach and clambered up the rocks, peering into every crevice. Nimai found an old nest with broken eggshells in it; Maroo found a little cave just big enough for a child to sit in and watch the changing sea, but no good for a home. It was Otak who discovered the cave. A narrow entrance opened out into a wide, high chamber. Bones and a broken shell necklace told them that people had camped here before. The children were sent up to the cliff top to gather armfuls of heather for bedding. These were arranged around the main area and covered over with skins and furs.

A chilly breeze was blowing, but the encircling cliffs

kept the bay warm. The children took off their boots and trousers and ventured timidly into the sea, gasping with the cold shock as the sea ran rippling around their feet. They scampered back up the beach as the wave retreated, then ran to meet the next one. This time the water did not seem so cold. They paddled deeper.

Nimai shouted, "Look! People!" She was pointing out to sea.

They all stared. Two dark heads had appeared above the waves. As they watched, another bobbed up beside them, and then another.

Areg came and squatted beside the children. "They are the Seal People," he said. "Call them a greeting."

Otak called and waved his arms. Nimai copied him. The seals bobbed with the waves but made no response.

"They are coming nearer!" said Maroo.

The children began to wade out, up to their knees. The sea sucked sand from around their feet. The seals moved gently away. When the children went back to the beach, the seals drew nearer again.

All that day the Seal People watched as the families worked on their home, making it warm and secure. Sometimes a bolder one would come close to the shore so that they could see its broad, whiskered face and mild round eyes; but as soon as anyone went near it, the seal would disappear under the water, to re-emerge farther out.

The next day Vorka sat engraving a seal on his bone amulet while the others made necklaces. Maroo knew that the cone-shaped whelk shells brought good luck; she helped her mother collect tiny ones to make a necklace for the new baby. The beach was full of different shells. Maroo found tiny pale pink fans, long brittle shells like flat pieces of bone, dark blue mussels, and spiraled cones. They could be arranged in endless variations to make rings for wrists, necks, and ankles.

Sticking to the rocks the children found ridged conical shells that would not come off. Areg said they were limpets. He knocked one sharply with a stone. It fell off into his hand, and they saw that it was not just a shell but a living creature. It was good to eat, Areg said.

The children soon learned to dislodge the limpets by themselves. They took them to Old Mother, who soaked them all day on a shelf of rock halfway up the cliff where a freshwater stream ran down. The next day she sent Maroo to fetch water in the stag's-head bowl and put the limpets into it. Then she pushed her cooking stones into the base of the fire, and, when they were hot, dropped them into the bowl to cook the limpets. They tasted good. The children collected them eagerly, day after day, and never tired of them.

Most days the Seal People bobbed in the waves just out of reach and watched them. The men would not hunt the Seal People. The sea was desperately cold, and they feared and respected it. They did not swim and had never learned to make boats. There was plenty of varied food to be had on the shore: limpets, winkles, and crabs, and hares and lemmings on the cliff top. Maroo liked to lick salt from the rocks. The women scraped it off and used it to flavor the cooked meat. They gathered seaweed and cooked it with the hot stones, and picked berries and green shoots growing on the cliffs.

It was now high summer. Although the sea breeze blew fresh, the sun was hot, and the people were able to take off their heavy furs and wash in the rock pools and bask on the warm sheltered beach. They laughed to see each other's white bodies contrasted with the dark weather-reddened faces and hands.

One hot day Otak and Maroo took Rivo and went exploring farther along the rocky part of the beach, where they found a large, deep rock pool. The children lay on their stomachs on the rocks and gazed into the pool; there were tiny crabs in it, and transparent shrimps, and a sea anemone waving its little sinister arms. Suddenly Rivo splashed into the pool, scattering the wildlife to the stony depths and barking joyously. The children shrieked with laughter. Rivo swam to the other side, jumped out, and shook water all over them.

Maroo wanted to swim like Rivo. She leaped into the pool and threw herself forward, but her legs sank. Otak threw a stick into the pool, and Rivo dived in again, splashing Maroo as he retrieved it.

"See!" exclaimed Otak. "He fetched it! He could fetch small animals for a hunter. And he could help track the game. His nose is better than mine. Remember how he sniffed out those voles yesterday?"

Maroo stood up in the pool, streaming water. "Let's tell Father," she said.

Areg and Vorka were sitting together on the beach. Vorka was making a necklace for Nimai, and Areg was binding a new head onto his spear. The children explained their ideas while Rivo frisked beside them. Vorka, as they had expected, could not see the need for a dog, but even Areg laughed and said, "A hunter would be better off without that dog of yours. Look at him! He's too jumpy and he barks too much."

Maroo's spirits drooped.

Areg saw their disappointment and relented. He put down his spear. "Rivo must learn to be still when you command him, and he must learn not to bark," he said.

He showed them what to do, pushing the dog's haunches down and commanding him to sit. Rivo did not understand. As soon as Areg took his hand away, he leaped up and put his paws on Areg's chest and wagged his tail. The children laughed.

"He will learn," Areg said.

The children set themselves to teach Rivo. They soon had a little success. Sometimes Rivo would sit when they commanded him; often he would not, but they were certain that he understood even if he would not always obey. Stopping his barking was more difficult, but Otak knew that a dog that barked was no good to a hunter, and he was determined to stop it. He would smack Rivo's nose when he started to bark, and reward him with tidbits of food when he was quiet.

Areg watched the training with approval, but the other men were skeptical; they thought Areg was indulging the children.

The summer reached its zenith and began a gentle decline. Sometimes, when Maroo sat daydreaming in her tiny cave halfway up the cliff, the sun would beat so hot upon her that she would take off her fur jacket, but when she stepped out of the cave the wind would strike cold again.

Several times Maroo saw her mother stop what she was doing and breathe deeply. The baby would soon be born. Tikek chose a place at the back of the cave and made it cozy with layers of heather and a pile of furs. Tikek was ready, but the baby did not come. They waited, day after day, but although the baby kicked impatiently it still did not come.

Autumn was advancing. There was a chill in the air and the sea looked restless, echoing the mood of the people who knew that they should be on their way to the autumn hunting grounds before the long cold set in. Tikek knew this too, but she would not move now, with her place ready and the knowledge that the birth was near.

The time came early one morning. The baby had not moved for a day, and that night Tikek said, "It will be soon." Toward dawn Old Mother roused everyone and sent them away, all except Avni. The men climbed up the cliffs, taking Rivo and the children with them to look for tracks of lemmings and seabirds. But Maroo left the others and went to sit in her own little cave overlooking the cold gray sea and sky. The sun was sleeping still below the sea, and only the faintest gray light hovered on the horizon.

Maroo looked at the paling stars, noting their positions. She knew the names of all the stars, and their movements, but not the significance of their positions at the time of birth. Old Mother understood those things, and would know what the future held for a baby born at this hour.

The stars faded as light crept across the sky. The cliff came alive with the rustlings of birds and voles. Maroo could hear faint sounds from below: Old Mother and Avni talking, an occasional moan from Tikek. She listened intently. She longed to know what it was like to give birth; in a few more summers she might be part of the mystery herself.

The rising sun flashed on the sea, and golden light spilled over Maroo in her little cave. At the same moment the quiet was split by a wild calling from the throats of Avni and Old Mother, telling everyone that the child was born and was alive.

Maroo sprang to her feet and slithered down the cliff, determined to be there first.

=7=
The Ibex Hunt

OLD MOTHER AND AVNI were still calling when she reached the cave. Old Mother smiled and led her inside. Tikek was lying on the furs, her hair draggled and stuck to her face with sweat. She was too tired to speak, but her eyes were bright. The baby lay in the crook of her arm, asleep. Maroo stared at its crumpled, old man's face.

"It is a son," Old Mother said, as proudly as if she had borne it herself.

The men and children arrived and crowded around. Nimai pushed her way to the front, and Areg began at once to make up a new song. Old Mother shooed them all away, all except Avni and Maroo, who was allowed to stay crouched beside her mother, watching the baby. Outside she could hear Nimai's voice and the tapping of Areg's fingers on the drum.

The next day Tikek got up. She made a sling for the baby from a strip of hide tied around her body, and carried him on her back, feeding him whenever he cried. Mostly he slept. Nimai was sent to find soft leaves and moss to tuck inside his fur wrap and keep him dry, and that became her daily task. Tikek soon began to recover her strength, but she was still too weak to travel. Maroo knew that they should have been on their way west already. The mornings were cold now, and the last of the fruits and berries had been picked.

That night the adults talked together and decided that Sovi's group should leave the next day and that Areg's group would follow in their trail a few days later.

They had a feast of lemmings roasted on sticks over the fire, and the next morning Sovi's group rolled up their furs and took the trail to the west. The children clambered to the cliff top and watched until they were out of sight.

It was two days later that Areg's group took up the trail. The children were sorry to leave the beach. They ran about by the edge of the sea until the last moment, watching the Seal People bobbing in the choppy water; they were far out now, and the sea was breaking around them in tufts of white foam. Areg's shouted command brought the children running up the beach with Rivo bounding beside them. Maroo took up her bundle. Somewhere inside it was a small bag full of shells, which she would spend the winter sewing onto a new fur jacket, using the traditional patterns that Old Mother had taught her.

Because Tikek tired easily, they traveled more slowly than the others and did not reach the site of

Sovi's first campfire until the middle of the second day. The distance between the two groups gradually increased, but every night they saw the smoke from each other's fires, and Sovi would leave signs and messages for Areg. Once, in Sovi's fire place, they found a pattern of sticks and stones that meant, "There is good fishing downstream by the flat rocks."

Areg and Vorka went to the place and caught three salmon, and that night they sent a signal to Sovi by fanning the fire with a hide so that the smoke went up in bursts. Sometimes Sovi would leave a drawing scratched on a stone; one simply told them, "We tracked a fine buck, but he got away," another warned them to beware of marshy land lower down the hillside.

Sovi's trail went high up into the mountains, and the way was often steep. Because Tikek was still weak, Areg turned off the trail and chose a lower path that made traveling easier. That night they found for the first time since the journey began that they could not see a signal fire ahead of them.

They had stopped on a large plateau with big tumbled boulders around that would make good shelters, and a high sheer rock wall to the northeast. Although it was sheltered, the place seemed unfriendly in a way Maroo could not explain. Perhaps it was just that they felt lonely without a sign from the other group. Areg made a tune on the drum, and they began to sing and clap. They started loudly, but the voices petered out and hands paused until only Nimai was still clapping.

"Ssh!" Tikek told her. Everyone was staring at the rock wall. Someone over there had been singing and clapping with them.

Areg clapped loudly and experimentally: *clap, clap, clap*. Back came the answer from the rock wall: *clap, clap, clap*.

There was silence. Maroo felt her hair lifting; she could smell fear; even Old Mother was afraid. Rivo stood erect, growling. They all turned to Old Mother, looking for guidance.

"It is a spirit," she said. "Sometimes a high rock like this is the home of a calling spirit."

"Will it harm us?" Vorka did not sound hopeful; Maroo wondered if he, too, sensed the atmosphere of the place.

"I don't know," Old Mother said, "but I have always felt afraid of them."

"Perhaps we should not camp here?" suggested Areg.

They looked around. It was dusk already, there were no other sheltered places near, and Tikek was very tired.

"We must stay here," Old Mother decided. "We will leave a gift for the spirit."

The men had a good catch of fish, speared earlier in the day. Areg took the two largest fish and carried them cautiously across the stony ground to the foot of the rock wall. He made a ring of pebbles and placed the offering inside it. Then he came back, glancing nervously over his shoulder.

"Now we must eat," said Old Mother briskly. They cooked the two remaining fish and broke them into several pieces. Old Mother also shared out dried meat and some dry withered berries. They were still hungry afterward; they had caught fish a few times but had not tasted fresh meat since they left the sea.

Old Mother tended the fire while Tikek suckled the baby and the two men made a rough shelter among some boulders opposite the high rock wall. Old Mother left the fire burning brighter than usual; they guessed it was meant to be a precaution against evil spirits, although she said nothing.

Maroo crawled into the tiny space where they all huddled together for warmth and rolled herself up in her furs. She lay with her face toward the entrance. Between her and the menacing rock wall was the flicker of the fire and the reassuring silhouette of Vorka, who was keeping the first watch. Above the rock wall she could see a strip of starry sky. One star was brighter than all the others: Irimgadu, the evening star. She thought of Old Mother, who was named Irimgadu after the star; Old Mother had said once that she always felt protected when she could see her star. Maroo fell asleep watching it.

She woke in the night and looked out. The darkness was absolute. She sensed that the weather had changed. All but one or two of the stars had been swallowed up by the night. The wind was angry and howled among the rocks above the shelter. There was another sound, too, a throaty animal rumbling. The fire had died down to red embers with worms of blackened wood twisting and falling into it; she could see nothing beyond its faint glow. She was frightened and curled up tight against Old Mother, hiding her eyes.

Almost at once, it seemed, she was awake again. The night had gone, leaving the sky starless and full of streaming clouds. It was early; the sun was still sleeping. The fire was a heap of gray ash. Vorka's place had been taken by Old Mother. Old Mother, who always woke early, preferred to take the last watch of the night.

It had been a cramped night, and everyone was stirring uncomfortably. Maroo found that her legs were numb; Rivo was lying across them. He trotted out when she moved.

Old Mother laid a hand on her arm. "See! The gift has gone!"

Maroo peered into the dimness at the foot of the cliff. It was hard to see yet, but she thought Old Mother was right.

Areg came out next. "I heard the spirit come," he said, "while I was watching in the night. Rivo was awake. He growled when the spirit came."

Maroo followed him as he went cautiously toward

49

the offering place to investigate. The ring of stones was broken, and the fish had been dragged out and eaten. There were no prints on the rocky ground, but there was a smell lingering: catlike, Maroo thought; lynx or cave lion.

Areg agreed. "The spirit came as a great cat," he said.

Maroo imagined a gigantic lynx with great yellow eyes and claws curved and gleaming like the new moon.

Areg led the way back to the camp. Vorka was outside now, and he and Areg made a circuit of the camp, "looking at the morning," as they called it. The children followed them, and the men pointed out to them the signs they must learn to recognize: a crevice in the rock where owls were nesting, betrayed by regurgitated balls of fur and feathers nearby. Areg picked one up and showed the children that the owl had eaten voles and a hare. In another crevice the smell of fox was strong.

Higher up, they found droppings: clumps of small black pellets. "Ibex," Vorka said, not aloud, but by making the ibex sign with his hands; even when they were not hunting, they avoided talking when possible. Old Mother had a saying, "The hunter who chatters will catch only carrion."

Further on, Otak spotted the print of a cloven hoof in some damp moss. The men were pleased with him. The droppings were everywhere: clearly a large group was grazing here. The men began to talk of a hunt. Maroo felt saliva run in her mouth at the thought of meat. But when they returned to the campfire, Old Mother was uneasy. Two men were not enough to hunt ibex, she said, and Sovi was too far ahead now to be called.

Vorka began to look doubtful, but Areg laughed away his fears. They were hungry for meat, and the signs of ibex were rich on the ground; perhaps the rock spirit was grateful for their gift and had brought the ibex to them?

"It is unwise," said Old Mother, "to hunt large game when the group is so small." But Maroo could see that the thought of meat tempted her; and perhaps Areg was right and the rock spirit intended it. At last she agreed. Areg was glad; he pretended to be an ibex and butted Nimai, who shouted with laughter. Vorka was won over by Areg's confidence, and they made ready at once, sharpening their spears and planning how and where to trap the ibex.

Otak wanted to go with them and bring Rivo, but the men said no. Even without Rivo they would not allow Otak to go. It was too dangerous. All Otak could do was to sit close by them and listen to their plans so that he could impress his sisters later with details of the hunt.

The children watched as Areg brought out two horns, one filled with red stuff and the other with black. The stuff was earth mixed with fat to make a paste. The brothers dipped their fingers in the paste and painted each other's faces with a pattern of stripes and diamonds. When Areg turned and looked at Nimai out of his new strange face, she backed away and clung to Maroo. Maroo laughed, but she, too, was a little afraid of the changed faces. The man was Areg and yet not only Areg; he had become an ibex.

The men took up their spears and began climbing higher up the mountain. Soon they were out of sight.

The camp was quiet without them. Otak found the horns of colored paste and began painting his face. The girls played quiet games, building tiny shelters with bits of bone, or rolling stones and knocking them against each other to see who could win the most. They dared not shout or laugh because when they did, the rock spirit shouted back.

The children climbed around and collected some withered fruits, a basket of nuts, and a few sticks of firewood. Maroo found mushrooms growing in a grassy patch where water ran down. She gave them all to Tikek, who was always hungry now because of the baby. The baby whimpered constantly for milk, and Tikek fed him, and in between times she mended clothes, while Old Mother put a new handle on a basket.

At dusk the men had not returned. Old Mother said, "It is nothing. They will sleep out and hunt again in the morning," but Maroo sensed her anxiety. She looked at the rock wall looming up dark and strange in the fading light and wished she had not given all the mushrooms to her mother.

There was nothing to offer the spirit except dried meat, and they had little enough of that, but Old Mother took some, remade the ring of stones, and placed it inside. Then they were each given a portion to eat, and water to drink from a spring higher up the mountain.

They crept under their shelter to sleep. Everyone was hungry. Maroo took the first watch, with Rivo beside her. Her stomach growled its protest as she sat chewing a hard root. Maroo was afraid. She sensed that something was wrong. The two women seemed anxious. The hunters might stay away at night, as Old Mother had said, but not when there was no man or strong young woman to protect the family.

She listened to the night, straining to hear any sound of the hunters. Perhaps they were near, in one of the little caves higher up. She heard the cry of an owl hunting, and the high piping of bats, and once she tensed in fear when she thought she heard a low, cat-like growl. Rivo stood up, ears erect, but the sound did not come again. There was no human voice, but then Areg and Vorka would not talk above a whisper, and they moved as softly as hares.

The owl hooted again, and from the rock wall its voice was thrown back mockingly. Maroo crouched close to the fire for comfort and poked at it with a stick, so that a shower of sparks shot up briefly and hid the wall. She longed for her watch to end, but it was not yet time to wake Otak. The moon was her guide to the time; when it reached the highest point of the ridge, she was to wake him.

Tonight the moon was newborn and gave scarcely any light. Irimgadu shone brighter. Maroo was comforted by the sight of Irimgadu; if the star had been hidden by cloud, she would have felt more threatened by the rock spirit. She was sure that the rock spirit was bad, even though it had brought them the ibex.

The baby cried, breaking the night's stillness. Maroo heard Tikek stirring and shushing the child. Tikek raised herself on one elbow. "Who is watching?" she whispered.

"Maroo."

The moon was still far from the highest ridge, but Tikek said, "You sleep now, Maroo. I will watch and wake Otak later. How is the night?"

"I heard an owl, and bats, and . . . perhaps a lion. . . . Irimgadu is bright," she added, unnecessarily.

She sensed Tikek's smile at that. "Good. Go to sleep."

Maroo patted Rivo and went into the shelter and changed places with her mother. The baby was already attached to Tikek's breast and sucking with little gasps of contentment. Tikek crawled out, holding him on one arm, and squatted beside the fire, and

Maroo settled into her space, where the furs were warm from her body. She was soon asleep.

She woke to the familiar sight of Old Mother fixing the bone pins in her coiled hair. The stones were heating in the fire, and Nimai was handing nuts around.

"You must search for the men," Nimai said importantly.

Maroo felt cold inside. She looked at Old Mother.

Old Mother turned around, and Maroo saw that she was afraid. "They should have returned," Old Mother said. "We must find them today."

She said no more, but dropped the hot stones into the bone bowl full of water flavored with herbs, then tipped the hot liquid into the drinking bowl and passed it first to Tikek. Tikek sipped and passed it back. Only when everyone had drunk did Old Mother tell Maroo to fetch a coil of twisted hide rope and Otak to fetch his spear. Tikek and Nimai would stay behind, she said, in case the men came back.

Old Mother led the way up the mountain, Maroo and Otak following, and Rivo running beside them. The trail was hard to find. The hunters were skilled and left few clues, but they all began casting about, and soon Maroo found a footprint in damp moss. Rivo sniffed at the footprint and trotted off fast, with his nose to the ground. "He has found the trail!" Otak whispered.

The three of them followed the dog, who ran on unchecked. The trail wound a long way among the high rocks, and all about were the prints and droppings of ibex. Once, as they reached the top of a hill, there was an abrupt clatter of hooves, and they saw the white rumps of several ibex darting away.

They went on, still following the dog. Rivo was some way ahead of them when he stopped. He seemed to be on the edge of a cliff. He looked back at them and barked. As they hurried toward him, Maroo thought she heard a human voice. They reached Rivo and looked over the edge.

The ground fell away steeply, forming a small cliff. Vorka was trapped halfway down. When he stood up they saw that his right arm hung oddly as if it were broken.

And then Maroo looked past Vorka and saw something else: the huddled shape of Areg lying at the foot of the cliff.

=8=
The Silent Drum

MAROO AND OTAK both began to cry. "Is he dead?" they asked Old Mother.

But Old Mother only said, "Fetch the rope."

Maroo, sniffing back her tears, uncoiled the plaited hide rope. Old Mother looked around for something to tie it to. The rocks were too big. A small birch, its top flattened and forced sideways by the wind, grew near the edge of the drop. Old Mother tested the short, slender trunk. Would it hold? She wound the rope around the tree several times and tied it firmly.

"We must all pull, too," she said, "in case the tree breaks."

She sent the rope sliding carefully down until it reached the ledge. Vorka was squatting, resting his right arm awkwardly on his knees. He picked up the end. They saw him fumbling with cold hands as he tied it around his waist. He stood up and signaled that he was ready.

Old Mother muttered, "If that arm is broken, he won't be able to climb."

But the three of them stepped back and pulled with all their weight on the rope as Vorka began the attempt. The tree creaked and bent. Almost at once they heard a cry of pain and the rope went slack. When they looked over the edge, Vorka was crumpled up, shaking his head and groaning.

"There is too much pain," Old Mother said. "The arm must be splinted first. I shall go down."

Maroo looked at the climb down. It was long, many times her own height, and dangerous, with few finger-holds: impossible for Old Mother. "Let me go," she said. "I can splint the arm."

Old Mother looked doubtful. "It must be done skilfully or there will be great pain and the arm will grow crooked," she said. "A hunter's right arm is a task for Irimgadu."

"You can't climb down, Old Mother," Maroo protested. "You will fall. Let me go. I've watched you splinting broken arms."

Old Mother hesitated a moment. Then she nodded. "You are right. You must go," she said.

Vorka had untied the rope, and Old Mother hauled it in. Maroo tied it around her own waist and carefully lowered herself over the cliff feet first, feeling for toe-holds in the rock. Otak and Old Mother stepped back, ready to brace themselves against the rope if she should slip.

Maroo moved cautiously down the first few steps. Her eyes came level with the cliff top and then, with the next feel and step down, passed below it. She felt panic-stricken. She clung with white, clenched knuckles to the rough rock, unable to let go. Looking down between her feet, she saw the upturned face of Vorka, still streaked with its hunter's patterns, far below. I'll fall and kill him, she thought. Movement seemed impossible. Her fingers were frozen to the rock. Vorka called up encouragingly from below, but the rock face looked sheer. Where would she put her feet? She heard Otak's voice from above: "Go on. The tree won't break. And we've got the rope."

She unstuck one hand and felt downward, at the same time finding a tiny space for one foot. Groping with the other foot, she found a hold, but there was nothing for her hands. Her nails scraped against the rock and she clutched at a tuft of moss that started to come away. She slithered down with a gasp, moss in her fingernails, and felt the rope tighten briefly before she found another hold.

Looking down, she saw Vorka much nearer. Now came a difficult part, where the cliff curved under before it reached the ledge, and she found herself hanging like a spider upside-down. When her feet had found a place, she had to let her hands go and swing quickly forward to avoid falling.

And then she felt Vorka's hand touch her boot. She was there. She dropped down onto the ledge. A shout of relief came from above.

Vorka hugged her against his left side.

Tears rolled down Maroo's face. From here Areg looked much nearer. He lay still.

"Is he dead?" Maroo whispered.

"I think he must be."

She felt Vorka's tears on her face. His skin looked gray under the red and black paint, and he was shaking with cold and pain.

"Let me see the arm," she said.

The ledge was small, and the two of them seemed to fill it. With difficulty Maroo maneuvered herself into a position in which she could splint the arm. It was broken just below the elbow. Vorka gasped in pain as she touched it. Maroo took from her pouch a bone digging stick and used it as a splint, tying it firmly in place with strips of leather. She made a rough sling from another strip and tied it across his chest. There were no other broken bones, but one of his ankles was bruised and painful. She saw that he would have trouble walking.

The problem of getting him off the ledge now filled her thoughts. The way down was nearer, and might be easier for him. There was an upright needle of rock on the ledge around which she could perhaps wind the rope. Vorka agreed to try, and they called up to Old Mother to let the rope down. Otak and Rivo had gone. They were already looking for an easier way down, Old Mother said.

Maroo wound the rope several times around the rock and tied it with a knot that would not slip. The free end she fastened around Vorka's waist. She watched him go over the edge. He moved slowly and very cautiously, using feet and one hand. Maroo thought that she could never have done it herself one-handed, but Vorka was a skilled climber, and the alternative was death. He reached the ground, panting, and limped toward the still figure of Areg.

Maroo pulled in the rope, untied it, and threw it down. She could not use it herself or the rope would have to be left behind, tied to the rock. She launched her feet over the side, bracing her weight against the rock face. The climb was not so difficult as the one she had just done, and she moved fast to overcome her fear, sliding down the last section and landing with a jolt. She noticed then, for the first time, the dead ibex lying at the foot of the cliff. She ran to Vorka's side.

Vorka had turned Areg over. There was blood matted in his hair and frozen to the side of his face. Maroo saw, without needing to touch him, that he was dead. Vorka crouched beside him in utter misery. The painted patterns on Areg's face were crisscrossed with lines of blood, and Maroo was frightened — it was like looking at a spirit.

She heard a sound of falling stones and looked up to see Old Mother scrambling down a path at the far end of the gorge. "Old Mother!" she shouted, and ran to meet her.

Old Mother took her hand as Maroo sobbed, "Father is dead. I'm frightened of his spirit."

They reached the body and squatted beside it.

"What shall we do?" Maroo asked.

Old Mother's face was wet with tears. "We will wait for your mother and the little ones," she said. "Otak has gone to fetch them."

While they waited, Old Mother gradually drew from Vorka what had happened: how he and Areg had hunted all day without luck and were about to come back to the camp, when, just as the light was failing, they saw a chance to surprise a group of ibex on the cliff top and perhaps drive some of them over the edge. If it had been familiar territory they would probably have succeeded, but they were in a strange place, and it was getting dark. An ibex fell, but Areg missed his footing in the half-light and fell too, and so did Vorka, who had sprung forward instinctively to try and save his brother as he went down.

Maroo listened, crouching beside Old Mother. But Vorka's words and the dead body of her father did not seem real. The change was too sudden. How could Areg, who had been so much alive, be dead?

The sound of Nimai's voice roused her. Nimai and Rivo were running toward them, followed by Otak and Tikek with the baby. They had brought all the hides and cooking things from the camp. Tikek gave the baby to Old Mother while she ran and fell to her knees beside Areg.

"Mother!" said Maroo.

But Tikek did not seem to hear. She began to wail, louder and louder. Her face was contorted.

Maroo felt frightened. She ran and shook her mother by the arms. "Mother!" she screamed again.

Tikek stopped and stared at her. Then she threw her arms around Maroo and they both began to cry.

Maroo had run out of tears when she felt Old Mother touch her arm, offering a bowl of hot water scented with herbs. The fire was blazing and the younger children were crouched beside it. Otak had been crying, but Nimai looked bewildered. Vorka was still cold and shaking. Maroo passed the bowl to her mother.

Tikek drank, and steadied her voice. "I brought the horns," she said.

Old Mother fetched the horns full of paint, and she and Tikek streaked each other's faces with black stuff, and then Tikek painted Maroo's face. Old Mother washed away the blood and the hunter's symbols from Areg's face, and painted it again with magic signs that would help him make his way in the spirit world.

The two women took antler picks and began to dig a shallow grave beside the stream, while the children erected the shelter. It was simply a lean-to against a crevice in the cliff; they would only need it for one night.

When the grave was ready, Maroo helped her mother and grandmother lift Areg into it and cover him up with soft hides. Tikek brought Areg's spear and laid it beside him, and Otak brought his harpoon. Then Maroo found the new drum, and the tears rushed to her eyes as she remembered the day they had celebrated its making. She offered it to Vorka, but he pushed it away.

"It will not speak to me," he said.

Reluctantly Maroo laid the drum, too, into the grave.

The women were bringing heavy stones, which they placed on Areg's chest and legs to keep the spirit from walking. There was no soft earth, so they began piling more stones over the grave. The women made a wailing repetitive sound as they worked, halfway between crying and singing. The children found themselves drawn in, and soon Maroo was wailing with a tear-streaked face as she helped pile up the stones. Only Vorka squatted silent and tearless beside the grave.

When they had completely covered Areg and made him safe from predators, they turned their attention to the ibex. Tikek sat down and fed the baby, and Vorka still squatted, shivering, beside the grave, but everyone else worked at skinning and cutting up the ibex. Soon there were chunks of meat sizzling on sticks over the fire. Old Mother offered Vorka a bowl of hot blood, but he shook his head.

"You are the hunter. It is your right," Old Mother insisted.

But Vorka only turned away and put his free arm over his face.

The women and children shared the blood.

"Perhaps he will eat later," said Old Mother; she did not seem worried, but Maroo thought Tikek looked anxiously at Vorka. Rivo seemed to sense that something was wrong with Vorka; he whimpered around him and licked his face.

They spent the rest of that day cooking and eating as much of the meat as they could. It was better to eat it than to have to carry it. There was no time to cure the skin, but Otak took the beautiful ridged horns to keep, and they used the bigger bones to burn on the fire, cracking them open and laying them with their ends in the flames. Everyone ate until full except Vorka; he would not eat at all, but just squatted with his arm over his face. Tikek cried and pleaded with him, but he would not respond to her.

"He will die," Tikek said desperately to Old Mother, but Old Mother said, "It is a sickness of the spirit. It will pass. Tomorrow we must be back on the trail."

That night Vorka still had not eaten anything, but Tikek managed to persuade him to come into the shelter and try to sleep. Once, toward dawn, Maroo woke when Old Mother was watching by the fire, and saw that Vorka had emerged from the shelter and was talking in a low voice to Old Mother, but she could not hear what they were saying. She could see the moonlight shining on the piled stones of the grave. A shiver of fear went through her and she looked away.

As soon as it was light they woke and took the shelter down, and Old Mother revived the fire and made drinks. She took some special herbs from her pouch and sprinkled them into the hot water and handed the bowl to Vorka. Maroo was relieved to see him drink.

"Is he well now?" she asked Old Mother.

"He will recover. He must," Old Mother said.

"Was it the rock spirit, do you think," Maroo asked, "that made them fall?"

"I don't know," Old Mother said. "But it is good that we are leaving this place. I wish we had never camped here. I wish I had forbidden the hunt."

"But we were hungry," said Maroo.

"We were hungry," Old Mother agreed.

Later, as they all clambered up the rocky cliff path, with the dog at their heels, Maroo looked back at the lonely mound of stones beside the stream and thought of her father. She saw him playing his drum, and squatting beside her on the sand and telling her about the Seal People, and coming into the cave last winter to give her the fox pelt that trimmed her boots. She remembered long ago being carried on his shoulders when she was little like Nimai; and she remembered watching him climb up the rock path with Vorka on his last hunt, out of her sight. It was hard to imagine time going on without him.

They walked all morning, and at midday they found themselves back on Sovi's trail. But now the trail was cold.

They sat down in the shelter of some rocks to rest

66

and eat. Maroo sat beside Tikek and watched her feeding the baby. Tikek smiled sadly and said, "He has a name now. He is Areg." Maroo nodded. It was good not to lose a name when the spirit fled. And Areg was a good name for a man, for it meant simply "hunter." It was then that she realized, with a shock, that they had no hunter, only a boy and a wounded man whose spirit was sick. I shall have to hunt, she thought, and Rivo — yes, Rivo will help us.

She told her mother of her thoughts, and Tikek smiled and hugged her, but Maroo saw that she was worried.

"Tomorrow," Tikek said, "we must make an offering to the Great Mother and ask for help on our journey. If the snows overtake us, we will not survive."

═9═
No Smoke

WINTER SEEMED FAR AWAY in the days that followed. The weather was bright and sunny, even warm in the middle of the day, though the cold came quickly at sunset. They were following the course of a stream down from the mountains. Sometimes, standing on a high point of rock, they could see water leaping down the mountainside, springing from rock to rock in a turmoil of white foam, to join the Winding River on the plain below. And there below, like another river, a brown river moving slowly across the plain, were the deer, traveling west like the people.

Only there were no other people to be seen. They were still on Sovi's trail, finding his camp sites and signals, but the trail grew colder every day. Sovi was moving away faster than they could travel. Even when they stood in a high place overlooking the plain and scanned the trail until it disappeared behind the next range of hills, there was no sign of Sovi's group, nor of any other people, and no answering smoke at dusk when they lit their camp fire. So the knowledge that they were late gnawed at the back of the adults' minds.

The children clambered about the hillsides, searching out grassy patches where mushrooms and toadstools sprang up in big clusters overnight. They filled baskets and made a feast of them, eating handfuls raw or grilling them on sticks over the fire. The rivers brimmed with fish, and Otak grew more skillful at spearing them.

Vorka gradually recovered his spirits and began to eat and talk, but he could not hunt, nor even do much to help put up a shelter. With Vorka's injury and Tikek's tiredness and the demands of the baby, they progressed slowly. They knew that unless Sovi had decided to wait for them, they would not see smoke from another fire until they reached the autumn hunting grounds.

"He would be unwise to wait for us," Old Mother said.

Maroo knew she was right. To survive one must be ruthless, or risk the loss of many more people.

By the time they reached the plain, the weather had changed. The days were gray and darkness came early. Once a flurry of snowflakes reminded them of the danger they were in. It was as if winter were a giant striding behind them, his shadow already looming. They traveled as fast as they could, stopping only at dusk to eat, and setting off the next day as soon as it was light enough to see. For shelter at night they used crevices, rocks, or bushes, and one night they simply scraped a hollow in the ground and huddled under the skins and furs. Last winter Tikek had made ready for the baby a little fur jacket and hood. Wrapped in this and carried tucked inside her fur jacket, he stayed warm and safe.

The deer flowed by on either side of the Winding River. All day, every day, they passed inexorably along their ancient trail, each animal's hooves making a brisk snapping sound that became a great clamor as the hordes passed by. They moved slowly; like the people, they were seeking out mushrooms in the damp places. Vorka watched them in deep frustration. Here was meat for the taking, and he was unable to hunt.

Otak and Rivo became hunters of small game. Once Otak killed a lemming with his sling, and sometimes he speared fish, but more often Rivo would catch hares or marmots and bring them to Otak. Otak always rewarded him with a share of the catch, no matter how small it was or how many people it had to feed; he knew it was worthwhile training the dog to hunt with him. Sometimes Rivo would go off on a hunt of his own, bringing nothing back, yet showing no signs of hunger. Once he disappeared for nearly two days, and the children were sure they had lost him, but at dusk on the second day he trotted into their camp and lay down by the fire as if he had never left it.

"He knows he belongs to our hearth," Otak said.

They were not the only hunters on the move. Often they saw packs of dogs running alongside the deer, trying to isolate a weak animal. When Rivo heard the dogs, his ears would lift and his whole body quiver. Maroo and Otak kept a close hold on him at these times. They were afraid that he would go back to the wild if he met up with his own kind.

Once they saw the dogs make a kill. A young deer was separated from its mother and ran off, terrified, in the wrong direction, away from the herd. The dogs bounded after it and soon ran it down. The children saw the leader spring and heard the deer scream as it fell. The screams stopped when the dogs closed in and tore it to pieces.

Maroo and Otak had watched with interest, impressed by the dogs' tactics.

Otak said, "We should have taken that meat. We could have driven off the dogs."

"With fire?"

"Yes."

But the chance did not come again, and they lived mainly on roots and fungi, and the occasional small animal.

The Great Plain seemed endless, and they were utterly alone, except for the deer and the creatures that hunted them. The moon had been newborn when they left the cliff where Areg died, and it was new again when the first snow came. The night before there had been no sign of the moon nor of any stars; all afternoon the sky had been heavy with unshed snow. They camped, at Old Mother's insistence, in a sheltered space between some large boulders, using deerskins as roof cover. When Maroo looked out in the morning, it was to a white world.

The sun, swollen to monstrous size, had turned red and hung low in the sky. Its light made the snow crystals glitter with specks of rainbow color. Maroo felt the firm surface of the snow with her finger; she pressed, and it crumpled downward. The snow near the entrance was pure, with not a dent upon it except Maroo's fingerprint, but only a spear throw away it had been trampled by a trail of hooves.

The deer were passing slowly, searching for food. Maroo saw one animal stop and paw at the snow until it had cleared a grassy patch, where it began foraging for mushrooms. The deer's coat looked dark against the blinding snow; its warm breath hung on the icy air in a cloud.

The snow was not deep, but later that day it snowed again, driving them to seek shelter early. Nimai cried; she hated the snow in her face, so Maroo had to carry her. They saw the dog pack again, a little way ahead of them, nipping and worrying at the deer, this time without success.

Next morning it was still snowing, and they stayed late in their shelter until it stopped. By the following day the snow was thawing and the ground was wet and slushy, showing big patches of green. That was the day Maroo saw the ptarmigan. The birds were up on the slope above the overhang where the family was camped, pecking at leaves and berries among the short grass. A few were still flecked with their gray autumn plumage, but others were almost completely white.

Maroo signaled to Otak. He came with his sling and crept cautiously toward the flock. Maroo watched him. If Areg had been alive, if Vorka had been uninjured, she thought, there might have been three or four birds roasting over the fire tonight; but at least there was a chance of one.

Otak's sling was made of a forked antler tine and a strip of well-chewed stretchy hide. He fitted a pebble into the hide, drew it slowly back, and let go.

The stone sang. The birds erupted into flight, loud, clapping wingbeats taking them rapidly aloft; the air was full of their crackling cries. Otak leaped and waved the sling: one bird was down. Maroo climbed up to the grassy ledge. The bird lay stunned. It was a male: pure white except for his scarlet eyebrow feathers and a black border around his tail.

Otak killed the bird with a stone and carried it proudly to the hearth place. The two women and Vorka praised him. Maroo plucked the bird, saving the feathers. The larger ones might decorate a headdress, and the soft ones would make the stuffing for a doll for Nimai.

Old Mother gutted the ptarmigan, stuffed it with nuts and mushrooms, and wrapped it in leaves to roast in the fire. It was little enough to share among all of them that evening, but welcome. They took off their sodden boots and dried them around the fire. Otak's feet were painfully cold, and Old Mother found that one of his toes was almost frozen. She chafed it back to life, tut-tutting at him for not having complained before. "A little longer, and you would have lost that toe, and before long, your foot," she said, and told them all a cautionary tale of a boy who had walked till his feet were frozen and had died as a result. Otak and Maroo exchanged a glance and smile behind her back; they had heard all Old Mother's warnings many times.

Before they reached the White Mountain, the first blizzard came. Old Mother predicted it the night before, when they heard the wind screaming past their shelter and felt the icy sting of the air. She and Tikek went out after dark and laid extra stones around the edges of the skin covering and tied down loose flapping ends. All night the shelter tugged and strained at its anchorages as if it longed to join the wild racing of the wind.

By morning the blizzard had begun. The wind shrieked, drowning their voices as they struggled to dismantle the shelter. Tikek had wanted to stay, but Old Mother refused. They must keep moving, she said; the blizzards would only get worse. There was an outcrop of rock half a day's walk away, and Old Mother planned to bring them to it by nightfall. Maroo knew the place: it was large enough to provide shelter from the wind, but a tiny landmark in the vastness of the plain. How would they ever find it in the blizzard?

"We may not find it," Old Mother admitted, "but we will try."

The rocks were due west. There was no sun, nothing to guide them except a natural sense of direction. Old Mother's instinct was particularly sure. She led the way.

That day was the longest Maroo had ever endured. Hour after hour they trudged slowly on with the bitter snow-laden wind stinging their faces and slicing through their heavy clothes. Maroo, her back and arms aching from carrying Nimai, was scarcely conscious of anything but the need to go on, one foot after the other, over and over again, until they stopped in numb weariness. There was no sheltered place to light a fire, so they ate cold dried meat and drank melted snow. Hunger was their only guide to the passage of time. Maroo did not know how long they had been walking when she put Nimai down to rest her arms and asked Old Mother if they could have missed the rocks.

Old Mother had stopped too, to concentrate on renewing her sense of direction and time. "I think we are near the place," she said. She took off her backpack and gave it to Maroo. "You take this for a while," she said. "I will carry Nimai."

Maroo gratefully took up the less awkward weight of the pack. The family drew together again with Old

Mother in the lead and Vorka at the rear. Maroo and Otak were in the middle. Rivo trotted beside Otak.

Maroo, squinting through half-closed eyes, saw nothing but whirling snowflakes, but before they had gone much farther she heard a shout from Old Mother: "I see the rocks!"

A few steps on, and Maroo saw them too: the shape was familiar to her, for she had often camped by these rocks before, but never in such bad weather. The place was simply a pile of large boulders standing the height of two men, with a few wind-cropped trees growing nearby.

The family walked around the rocks until they reached the sheltered side. At once the battering of snow and wind was cut off; the relief was enormous. Maroo, slipping the pack from her shoulders, felt that she could not have walked another step.

There was a large crevice between two of the boulders which would serve as a shelter for the night, but a wedge of sky showed at the top; the space would have to be roofed with skins. Otak and Maroo climbed up the rocks and stretched a hide across the gap, weighting it down with stones that Tikek and Old Mother found and passed up to them. The wind was so fierce on top of the rocks that they were almost blown off, and the hide kept flapping back over their faces, but at last they got the stones in place. With the roof made, everyone crowded into the small space, and Old Mother unrolled another hide and pulled it over them to serve as a makeshift doorway.

It was a cold, comfortless shelter without fire or space to move. All night they sat huddled together for warmth; no one slept much except the baby and Rivo.

Toward morning Maroo dozed off, wedged between Otak and Old Mother. She woke cold and stiff, to find that part of the roof cover had blown away and her jacket was encrusted with snow. Looking up, she saw that it was day. The snowstorm still raged, as savage as ever. To her shame, she felt herself beginning to cry.

"I can't bear another day like yesterday," she sobbed as Old Mother began sharing out the dried meat, giving a piece to everyone, even the dog.

"If today is like yesterday," Old Mother said, "we will have to stop and build a snow house until the blizzard is over." She looked around at the circle of cold, pinched faces, red-eyed from lack of sleep. "But if we can find the strength, we should walk for one more day."

Maroo sniffed. "Why can't we build a snow house now?"

"Listen," Old Mother said kindly, patting her shoulder, "if we stop, we may never move again. We have hardly any food left. We can't hunt in the storm. Once we stop, our only hope will be that the storms will end before we starve to death. I want to bring us as far as possible on our way before we give in to the blizzard. Do you understand now?"

Maroo wiped her face with her gloved hand. "Yes," she said humbly.

The family were ready to go. Tikek tucked the baby snugly inside her jacket and took up her bundle. Vorka and Otak lifted their loads. Maroo hoisted Nimai onto her shoulders and stepped out into the tearing wind.

That day the sky never lightened, and the thick flurrying snowflakes never ceased to fall. It was worse than the day before; they were hungrier, less hopeful, and exhausted from lack of sleep. Maroo had lost all sense of direction; she stumbled on, head bent against the knife-edge wind, following the small, hunched shape of her grandmother trudging ahead.

They stopped once, to melt snow under their jackets and drink it, chew a small piece of meat each, stamp their frozen feet, and brush the snow from the wolverine fur that framed their faces. Then the long march began again. As the sky darkened in the afternoon, the shrieking of the wind grew louder. The snow flying into their faces came faster and harder. At last, when she thought she could not take another step, Maroo saw Old Mother halt. The family crowded around.

Old Mother brushed the snow from her hood. She

was so cold that her jaw had gone rigid, and at first she could not speak. She took off a mitten and rubbed her face until the muscles relaxed. Then she said what they all expected: "We must stop now and build a snow house and wait until the blizzard is over."

═10═
Old Mother's Decision

MAROO HAD NEVER NEEDED to make a snow house before, but all the children had been taught how to do it and had practiced by making tiny houses for their dolls in the snow outside the winter cave. Now the family worked quickly, in spite of fatigue. Old Mother and the children cut and shaped the blocks, and Tikek and Vorka built them up and sealed the joints. Gradually they curved the walls inward to make a low domed house similar in shape to the huts they made from branches in summer, but much more solid.

When the round shape was finished, they built an entrance tunnel with a bend in it to keep out drafts. Then they crawled in, one after the other, and Old Mother made new fire. She twirled the bow-drill in its groove until a wisp of smoke came that could be fed with dry tinder from her pouch. She built up the fire with twigs and bones. The flames grew, sending huge shadows leaping around the white walls. Tikek began to unpack the hides and furs and spread them around the sides of the hut. Old Mother sat down on them with a groan, joking about the pain in her old bones, but Maroo knew the pain was real; she had never seen her grandmother look so old and tired before.

Tikek gave out the food, a handful of nuts and roots each, and some raw mushrooms. They ate ravenously, and Nimai cried for more.

Old Mother went to her pack and took out a few slivers of dried meat. "This is the last," she said solemnly, "but we will eat now and live, and trust that the Deer Spirit will bring us good hunting."

They shared out the meat and ate it, and drank melted snow. By this time the temperature in the snow house had risen, and Maroo was glowing with a warmth she had not felt since the brief summer. She basked in the warmth and felt her muscles lose their tension; she took off her soaked boots and clothes and put them to steam by the fire.

"I wish we could stay here," she said.

"If the blizzards go on, we may stay here forever," Old Mother said grimly.

For two days the blizzard roared, and they did not leave the snow house. There was nothing to eat; Nimai cried continually, and Maroo felt dizzy with hunger. Only the baby thrived. On the second day, when Nimai woke crying, Old Mother gave her a root to chew. Maroo's stomach was jealous, but, unlike Nimai, she understood that there was no food. Nimai sucked ravenously at the root.

Rivo twice attempted to go out and hunt, but each time the blizzard drove him back. He grew wild-eyed and snappish, and Tikek was afraid he might attack Nimai. She made Maroo and Otak tie him to the heavy bundle of hides in the entrance tunnel. For a while Rivo dragged at the rope and gnawed the hides, but weakness gradually overcame him and he lay dozing with his nose on his paws.

The snow house was warm, and they slept much of the time. When the hunger pains became too bad for sleep, they squatted around the fire, feeding it with the last of their store of wood, and drinking melted snow.

On the third day when Maroo woke she was surprised to see that Old Mother was still asleep. But Otak was stirring. "Let's look at the morning," he said.

They put on their jackets and boots and crawled out, blinking. The blizzard had gone, leaving clear, bright daylight. They stood up and looked around. Birds' claw prints and the track of a hare crossed the snow. A little way off, the hare's prints ended in a scuffle. There were no other prints — an owl had taken it, Maroo guessed. Raising her eyes higher, she saw the grazing deer, the river, and the distant hills.

"Otak!" she said. "Look!"

She pointed at the horizon, which showed clearly the long familiar shape of the White Mountain. It was not one peak, but a long range, its length making the summit look deceptively low. Against the pale sky the snow-covered heights looked impassable to Maroo; it was hard to believe there was ever a trail across them.

Otak, in spite of two days without food, jumped up and down. The end of their journey was now in sight. He called out, "Mother! Old Mother! Vorka! Come and see!"

Vorka and Tikek came out. They were relieved to see the White Mountain, but Tikek was still anxious. Burdened as they were, it might be nearly half a moon's journey in bad weather around the foothills of the White Mountain.

Old Mother came out last. Maroo noticed that she was pale and moved stiffly. Tikek took her by the arm. "See, Old Mother, how near we are. The White Mountain is no more than a day's walk from here."

But Old Mother shook her head. "We may reach the White Mountain, but we will never reach the hunting grounds now. Winter has overtaken us. We are too late," she said.

In the silence that followed these words they all heard the screams of an animal in pain. It came from the fringe of the herd of reindeer. They saw dark shapes flying past and heard the scream come once more: the dogs had caught a deer.

At once Maroo and Otak remembered their plan. Maroo caught Rivo and tied him up in the snow house. Otak ran and fetched two torches and plunged them into the fire. The ends had been coated with pitch, which flared up and burned steadily.

"Come!" Otak called. "Bring knives. We'll get a deer!"

Old Mother stayed in the snow house with Nimai and the baby, but the others raced across the plain to the place where the dogs were ripping at the deer's carcass. The torches trailed plumes of smoke as they ran; Otak held one and Maroo the other.

There were six dogs. They looked up and snarled menacingly from bloodstained muzzles as the children approached.

"Go! Go!" Maroo shouted, brandishing the burning torch at the nearest dog. It flinched, but came back growling. One dog began to drag away the deer's haunches, which had been torn off. Another leaped at Otak's torch, near his hands, where there was no fire, and clamped its teeth on it. Maroo thrust her blazing torch toward the animal; it let go and fell back, whimpering. Before it could recover she lunged at it again, and it turned tail and fled. Another dog followed it.

Otak ran, shouting fiercely, after the dog that had taken some of the meat, while Maroo thrust fire at the other three, who were darting in and ripping at the deer. Maroo sprang forward, straddled the remains of the dead animal, and beat back every attempt by the dogs to touch it. At last they sensed that they were beaten; they turned, whining, and trotted away. Maroo yelled in triumph and chased them across the blood-trampled snow.

Otak came back, dragging the mangled haunches. Tikek and Vorka ran forward with knives, and soon the meat was cut up and taken back to the snow house, where Old Mother was building up the fire.

Much later, when some of the meat had been eaten and everyone was full and warm, Old Mother said, "That was done well, children. You have saved all our lives."

Maroo glowed with pleasure.

Old Mother looked stronger now. Her eyes were bright again. "We can go on now for a little while," she said, "but the meat will not last long, and we will die if we follow the trail around the White Mountain."

"I can get meat again!" Otak insisted confidently.

"No," Old Mother said. "We will not often be so lucky. But you have shown that you are quick-thinking and strong, you and your sister. I have a plan. The trail around the White Mountain is too far, but there is a trail over the top of the mountain, though it is many years since anyone followed it."

Maroo heard her mother draw in her breath as if to speak, and then keep silence at a glance from Old Mother.

"The trail is a hard one," Old Mother continued. "There are glaciers and steep climbs, and —"

"The mountain spirits," Maroo said, wide-eyed, more to herself than Old Mother.

"The mountain spirits," Old Mother agreed. "Offerings will need to be made. Now, listen: I am an old woman and my legs are stiff; Vorka is injured, and your mother has the baby and Nimai; all this would delay us. Only two people are young and strong enough to cross the mountain: you and Otak."

At this Vorka gasped in amazement and Tikek cried out, "No! Not alone!"

"Maroo and Otak must go alone and fetch help," Old Mother insisted, "or we shall all die."

Tikek looked horrified. Old Mother made with her hands the sign that meant, "There is no choice," but Vorka exclaimed passionately, "There is no need for me to stay here, Old Mother! The bones have set. I can use my arm. If anyone goes alone, it should be me."

"Your arm is still weak, Vorka," Old Mother said gently. "You can't hunt — not well enough to be sure of surviving."

Vorka pulled up his sleeve and showed how he could move the arm. But Maroo saw that the muscles were wasted, and she knew that he could not yet use his spear or harpoon.

Vorka flushed. "Then let me take the boy," he said. "You can't send the children alone. Let me take Otak. He can hunt well."

"Yes, let me go! I'm not afraid!" Otak exclaimed eagerly.

Tikek turned on her son like a wild animal, tears

rolling down her face. "Be quiet!" she shouted. "Don't talk such nonsense. I won't let you go!"

She spoke furiously to Old Mother: "I have lost Areg. Must I lose my children too?"

Old Mother tried to comfort her. "We have to make a choice, Tikek. Only the Great Mother knows which is the right choice. I am telling you what I think is wisest. Vorka can't use his spear, but perhaps he can get food. If he can, we need him here to help us." She turned to Vorka: "You would not leave women and children alone and unprotected on the plain?"

Vorka sighed and looked away with a gesture of resignation. Tikek sobbed quietly.

Maroo sat close to her mother. "Don't be afraid. I'll take care of Otak," she said.

Otak himself seemed unaware of his mother's distress. His face was alight. "I shall hunt," he said. "Hares, and lemmings — maybe even a lion —"

"No!" said Old Mother sharply. "There must be no foolishness. You must go cautiously. If one of you is injured or lost, the other must leave him or her and go on alone. One must survive. Do you understand?"

"Yes," both children said.

Otak was quiet now, in awe of Old Mother.

Maroo looked around at the family. Tikek's tears and Old Mother's solemn words were frightening, but when she caught Otak's eye and saw the suppressed excitement in him, she knew that underneath her fear she felt the same. Spirits, lions, glaciers — she would rather face any danger than stay in the snow house waiting for rescue. Already she longed to be on her way.

=11=
The White Mountain

OTAK AND MAROO sat with Old Mother on the sleeping bench, listening as she told them how to find the trail across the White Mountain, scratching symbols in the ice and making them memorize the route, step by step.

She warned them again and again to be careful on the glacier, to make offerings to the mountain spirits before they attempted to cross it, to feel ahead with a staff before putting a foot down, above all to go slowly. The plateau at the top of the glacier, she said, would be colder than anything they had ever known; they might need to build a snow house to survive the night. After that, a day's walk should bring them to the Pass of the Spirits. There was a great cave above the pass.

"You will be afraid when you reach the cave," Old Mother said, and Maroo felt a prickle of fear at her back already, as if the mountain had reached out to her. "Don't linger there. Beyond the cave you will be on the eastern slope of the mountain, and when you look down you will see the Crossing Place."

"Can we take Rivo?" Otak asked.

All this time Rivo had been lying asleep between the two children, his muzzle on Maroo's knee. No one had thought about him until now.

Old Mother considered.

"Yes," she said at last, "you must take him."

The children smiled at each other.

"If he stays here he will eat precious food, but if you take him he can hunt for himself. And if you find yourselves starving, you must kill him and eat him."

Maroo and Otak exclaimed together, "No!" but Old Mother said sternly, "You must be prepared for this. If you need to kill the dog to survive, you must kill him. It will be better to kill him than to take risks hunting larger animals."

Otak nodded; he knew this caution was meant for him.

"And now," said Old Mother, "the most important thing of all, Otak. Maroo is your leader; you must obey her."

Otak looked sulky.

"I have chosen Maroo as leader because she is the elder and also because I can trust her to be sensible and cautious," Old Mother said. "The mountain is dangerous. You must cross it softly and quickly, like the hare on new snow, before it feels that you are there."

Maroo was apprehensive, not only at the prospect of leading the journey, but also at the thought of controlling Otak. Would he obey her? He could be so silly. She began almost to wish they were not going. alone.

Later Old Mother told them all a story, the one that explained how the moon and stars were made, and Maroo forgot her worries for a while.

"You must remember the songs and stories," Old Mother said afterward. "Stories give you hope, even when the worst comes. A man might have a sharp spear and a full belly, but if he has lost hope, he will die. Now, let us divide the meat."

They still had most of the meat they had cut from the deer. Old Mother gave only a little to Maroo and Otak to carry with them, and kept the rest for the family, who would be waiting in the snow house.

Tikek and Vorka both protested. They wanted to give the children more of the meat, but Old Mother said, "No. We must stay here, and this meat must last us many days. The children can hunt and forage. You and the baby and little Nimai must survive." It was a hard decision, but they all knew in their hearts that it was right.

When Otak and Maroo had put away their share of the meat in a skin bag, Old Mother looked at what remained and held up her wrinkled hands: if they ate just enough to keep them from starving, she said, there was enough meat left to last them as many days as the fingers on both hands. That should give time for Maroo and Otak to reach the autumn camp and send rescuers to the snow house. But if anything, weather or accident, delayed the children, the family might starve before help arrived.

Her grandmother did not speak of it, but Maroo knew that if the meat was running out and no help was in sight, Old Mother would leave the snow house and walk away across the plain until she died of cold or was killed by hungry animals, leaving one less mouth to feed. And that decision, too, would be right, but Maroo did not want to think about it.

Otak carried, besides the bundle of furs on his back, his spear, staff, bolas, sling, and knives of different kinds. Maroo carried her staff and knives and also part of the fire from the snow house, smoldering inside a horn slung from her belt. Old Mother had captured the fire and had spoken spells over it that would keep the children safe. Maroo carried her own fire-making tools, but she was glad to be given part of Old Mother's fire; she knew it would be a good magic to have with her.

It was time to part. Old Mother made a drink of hot herb-flavored water, and they passed it around from one to another. They hugged each other and spoke confidently of meeting soon when Otak and Maroo brought help, but Maroo could see that the adults did not feel as confident as they sounded. She was glad at last to be trudging away from the snow house with Otak and the dog and looking back to wave, because the unspoken fears of the adults made her feel uneasy.

Each time they looked back, the snow house seemed smaller. At last it was invisible, blended with the snowy plain, and only the tiny waving dots beside it marked where it was. Even so, Maroo and Otak were not afraid of being unable to find it again. They were accustomed to noticing every landmark, even on a plain empty except for rocks and stones and a few stunted shrubs. More snow might cover up their own tracks, but they would still be able to lead the rescuers to the tiny snow house.

They walked fast all day, happy and excited. Rivo scampered around them, and they threw a bone for him to chase and bring back. The White Mountain grew steadily nearer, and it was good to be able to walk swiftly toward it, without the crying of Nimai and the slow pace of the women.

Tikek had said that the White Mountain was a day's journey away, but despite their late start the children reached its lower slopes long before nightfall and decided to climb up to a small plateau they could see above them, near the foot of the huge glacier. Old Mother had described it to them as a good place to make camp.

The ascent was easy enough at first. The path they were to follow led up beside a little stony stream that came clattering down from the edge of the melting ice. They had no choice but to stay close to the stream, for on either side was a thick tangled growth of stunted willows and creepers, difficult to walk through.

There were many small streams crisscrossing the rough ground, joining together and growing bigger as they ran down the mountainside. Some were so small that they could be stepped over. For the others, Maroo would look for an easy crossing place, with large, flat stones in the water. Sometimes they slipped; then, even through their boots, the water sent an icy shock to the stomach.

As they rose higher above the plain, the streams became smaller and more numerous, and there was a sharp new cold in the air. The ascent grew steeper all the time, and they tired quickly. The sun had begun to dip, and Maroo was feeling that she could walk no farther, when they reached the plateau.

They threw themselves down on the ground and leaned on their packs. Maroo scooped up water in a hollow horn, and they drank from it in turn.

Maroo looked down at the plain far below. The low sun had turned it into a place of shadowy hollows and sparkling mounds. Every clump of willow or birch stood out crisply and threw a long dark shadow. In the distance, on the far side of the river, a brown line was moving: deer, or was it bison? Deer: a pair of proud antlers had showed briefly against the sky. Far beyond the deer a great lake flashed fire at the sun.

Maroo tried to find the snow house. She followed with her eyes the trail she and Otak had made, back and back across the plain, but it became impossible to see, and she had to look for landmarks: clumps of trees or rocks. She found the spot where she thought the snow house must be, but could not see it. Then, just as she was about to give up and ease her aching eyes, she saw what she was looking for: a tiny column of smoke rising from behind a clump of dwarf birch. It looked indescribably far away, and as she pointed it out to her brother she felt, for the first time that day, lonely and a little afraid.

She looked behind her. Above their camp soared the glacier they must cross tomorrow. Half of it was blinding bright, the other half blue in the shadow of a peak. It was wide and trackless, yet Maroo could see that there was only one way to go: up to a pass on the horizon between two sharp peaks.

But now they had to make camp for the night. Otak gathered twigs for firewood, and Maroo blew Old Mother's fire gently back to life. They made a ring of stones and sheltered the fire with their bodies until it was red and crackling. Maroo watched it lovingly; it was her first hearth-place.

Old Mother had said there was an overhanging rock at the back of the plateau where they could shelter at night. Maroo found it and began to arrange the furs inside. They both went into their shelter and shared some of the meat, while the sun was swallowed by the approaching night and the plain below grew dark.

Now the smoke from the snow house was gone, and

they were quite alone. Maroo sensed the spirit of the mountain all around them. What were spirits? Why was the mountain hostile to people? The unanswerable questions made her more afraid. "Let's go to sleep," she whispered.

Otak nodded. She saw that he, too, was afraid, but trying not to show it. They crawled under the rock and huddled close together for warmth. Rivo blocked the entrance with his body. The night wind woke, and they heard spirit voices in it. Neither could sleep. They lay awake, whispering. Yet for all their fear of the night, they were not afraid of the journey ahead, and never doubted that they would survive it.

To banish the night fears they talked of the autumn hunting on the banks of the Great River, and of the friends they would meet there. There would be dancing and feasting if the hunting was good, which it could hardly fail to be with the deer passing in an endless stream along the trail so that a man could scarcely miss.

Otak, filled with the importance of their mission, whispered, "I shall be a hunter soon. Maybe next winter or the one after."

Maroo laughed. "You're far too young! You'll have to wait several winters, till you are as old as I am, or more. Even I would be too young."

It was Otak's turn to be superior. "You! You will never be a hunter. You will never see the deep caves."

He had touched on a subject that Maroo had always been curious about. She dropped her quarrelsome tone and whispered, "What do you have to do to become a hunter?"

"You know it's all secret."

"But you must have heard something."

Otak's voice, next to her ear, said softly, "It's to do with bulls and horses and the secret pictures in the deep caves."

"Do you have to kill a bull?"

"I don't think so. It's something even more frightening than that."

"How could anything be more frightening than that?"

"I don't know, but that's what they say."

They stopped whispering, but Maroo could tell from Otak's breathing that he was still awake, probably thinking about the ordeal of becoming a hunter. That part of the winter caves, the deep mysterious hunters' sanctuaries, was unknown to her and always would be. Her life lay in the outer caves, around the hearth-place. The making of fire and the rituals of birth and death would be the mysteries she would be admitted to, and from which Otak would be excluded.

And the dances . . . Maroo squirmed down further into her furs and thought about the dances: some, like the Sun Dance, were danced by the whole tribe, even the toddlers, and some were hunters' dances; but many belonged solely to the women and girls. She began thinking herself through the intricate movements of the Grass Dance.

Somewhere far down on the dark plain a long, rising howl broke the stillness of the night. A wolf, Maroo thought. Rivo woke and whined softly. Maroo patted his head; his rough fur comforted her. The night was cruel, but she knew they would be safe in the shelter till morning.

═12═
The Glacier

THE GLACIER LOOKED a smooth slate-blue in the dawn light. Maroo led the way, using her staff to prod the snow ahead of her before she set foot on it. She knew how unstable the glacier was; there could be vast crevasses under the firm-seeming snow.

"You must hold on to Rivo, and follow exactly in my footsteps," she told Otak.

The snow at the edge of the glacier was not so smooth as it looked; it was soft and powdery, dissolving under their feet to join the streams running down the mountain. As they moved on, it became firmer, but when Maroo looked back she saw their footprints like a row of small wells that would soon freeze over.

They went on, Maroo still moving ahead with her staff, prodding the snow to make sure it was firm. The snow was no longer soft and wet; it had hardened to a solid crust, or so it seemed, but they knew that the ice that looked so firm was slowly moving.

As they trekked in a long diagonal across the face of the glacier, Otak and Rivo followed obediently in

Maroo's footsteps. Rivo sniffed and whined at the tracks of a hare, and Otak wanted to follow them, but Maroo said no, there could be no hunting until they were on firmer ground. To her relief, Otak obeyed after a moment's hesitation, pulling the dog's lead tight and plodding reluctantly along behind Maroo.

By midday they were more than halfway to the pass between the two peaks that Maroo had seen from far below. She began to feel confident that they would soon be safe. Both she and Otak were hungry, but they would not stop to eat until they were across the glacier.

Maroo looked up and saw the pass easily within reach, though the way up was steeper. She stepped forward, with the staff in her right hand. The snow crumbled a little under her left foot, and she felt a jolting movement. Before she could leap away, she was thrown violently sideways, there was a roar of cracking ice, and she felt herself falling. She screamed, clawing at the crumbling snow as she plunged down into a crevasse, an avalanche of snow and ice falling in on top of her.

At last it stopped. She lay still, too bruised and exhausted even to open her eyes. A great weight seemed to be pressing her down, urging her to sleep. When she did at last force herself to open her eyes, she moved in sudden panic, realizing that she was buried under the snow and would soon suffocate.

She tried to stand up, but the lower half of her body was trapped. She was not even sure which way was up — perhaps she *was* standing. Her arms and hands had some movement in them. She began to push up frantically at the snow, which was fast hardening over her. She seemed to be buried up to her neck, and it took all her strength to free the upper half of her body.

As she worked, a faint sound came to her from above. At first she did not react to it, absorbed as she was in her fight for life; then the sound penetrated, and she realized it was a voice: her brother's voice, calling her name. Tilting her head back as far as it would go, she squinted up at a patch of bright sky with a silhouette of a head in it.

"Otak!" she tried to call, but only a hoarse croak came out.

Something else appeared in the patch of blinding sky: something dark hurtling down. Instinctively she cringed, but it was not falling snow, it was a rope of plaited hide. Maroo heaved desperately with her legs, but they would not move. She began to dig with her hands, faster and faster, knowing that soon she would freeze and it would be too late. At last she was able to move part of her legs; then she felt life in one foot. She threw herself sideways and rolled over, freeing one leg and then the other, and ending up kneeling on all fours beside the rope. She crouched there, panting.

Her brother was shouting at her from the sky above,

but the shouting did not seem real; it seemed to come from another world. "The rope!" Otak shouted. "Tie the rope!"

With a great effort Maroo shook off her exhaustion. She took hold of the rope and knotted it firmly around her waist. She felt a faint tug from above; was she ready? She doubted if she would have the strength to climb out, but she gave an answering tug on the rope, stood up, and braced herself against the side of the crevasse.

The rope went taut. Maroo began to claw her way up the wall of the crevasse, grunting with exertion. Several times the rope slackened, and she heard a cry of alarm from Otak. Otak was so much smaller and lighter than she was—how could he hold her? Her foot slipped, she jerked downward with a gasp of fear, Otak yelled, and she saw him clinging to the edge of the crevasse and heard Rivo barking. In desperation she dug toeholds in the hard snow with her boots and clambered up, releasing the strain on Otak.

She looked up and saw the sky growing larger. Otak was there, his face hanging like a moon in the patch of blue. He shouted encouragement, but he looked frightened. Only a little farther now. With what felt like the last of her strength, Maroo dragged herself up until her hands touched his. He seized her wrists. She hauled herself up and out, and lay shaking on the ice. Rivo's wet tongue caressed her face.

When she had recovered enough to raise her head, she saw that Otak had driven his staff deep into the snow and wound the rope round it as well as around his own body to help take the strain. He untied the rope, coiled it neatly, and replaced it in his pack. Then he dropped down beside her, and she realized that they were both overcome with shock.

They crouched there, trembling, for some time, too tired to move, till Maroo said shakily, "We must go on — we dare not be trapped here at night."

She found her staff lying at the edge of the crevasse and picked it up. They both lifted their packs. Suddenly Otak touched Maroo's arm and pointed upward. There, on the pass between the two peaks, a big buck ibex was standing, quite unafraid, watching them. As they looked up, it turned and vanished over the brow of the hill.

Otak fixed wide, frightened eyes on his sister. Maroo felt her heart fluttering.

"Was it a spirit?" Otak asked.

"Maybe."

"Father's spirit?"

Maroo's heart beat faster. A vision came into her mind of Areg dead with the heavy stones laid on him to keep his spirit from walking.

"No," she said hastily. "Why should his spirit come so far?"

"To be with us?"

"No," Maroo insisted. But Old Mother had said that the mountain was guarded by spirits, and Areg had been killed hunting an ibex. Firmly she put these thoughts out of her mind.

"We must go on," she repeated. "Whatever is up there, we must go on now."

══13══
Blizzard

THE IBEX HAD GONE; the way ahead was clear. By the crevasse where she had fallen, Maroo made an offering to the mountain spirits. She tossed into the deep hole some of the precious shells she had found on the beach. The loose snow at the edges crumbled and fell in upon them.

For the rest of that day they saw and heard nothing, only the tiring whiteness of the landscape and the rasping of their own breath. There were no more accidents, but by the time they reached the pass between the two peaks at sundown, they felt drained of all strength. Maroo had never been so tired before. The ache in her legs spread up through her entire body, and it was only willpower that kept her going. Even the bruises from her fall were nothing compared with the overwhelming tiredness. When at last they stopped and squatted down to rest, she felt that she would never be able to get up again.

The place where they now found themselves was desolate. The deadly cold breath of the glacier blew upon them, and Maroo felt the bones of her face beginning to ache and her jaw stiffening. How would they keep warm tonight? She looked around. They were on an uneven plateau scattered with rocky ridges. Flat, snow-covered tracks wound between the rocks; they looked like paths, but unlike any paths made by people, they meandered aimlessly, linking and doubling back on each other.

Nothing moved in all that empty whiteness, not even a bird. The way they must take led up toward a ridge on the horizon. What had looked like the top of the mountain had been only the first peak; she saw now that they had a long, slow climb ahead of them across rough country toward the high place that Old Mother had called the Pass of the Spirits.

A wet touch came on her cheek, another on her mouth: snow was falling again. She looked around for a sheltered place. There were no caves near, and the sky hung heavy with snow.

"We must make a snow house," she said.

A small moan came from Otak.

Maroo saw that he was dropping with weariness. "We must," she insisted.

"Can't we camp under that ledge?" he begged, pointing it out, but knowing the answer must be no.

Maroo did not bother to answer him. Instead she began shaping the firm snow into rough blocks with her gloved hands. When they were of more or less equal size, she used her stone knife to cut them into perfect blocks.

Otak began laying the foundation ring, but he was tired and worked slowly. Maroo had to stop and help him make a firm seal as he laid on the first block of the second layer. She laid a few more blocks, tilting them inward at just the right angle. Then she went back to her shaping and cutting. "You must help," she chided Otak wearily.

But Otak was not listening. He had seen something in the snow just beyond the building. He signaled to her to come and look. Rivo was beside him, sniffing at the ground.

There was no doubt about what they saw: the broad print with those rounded pads and deep curving claws. A cave lion. She squatted and sniffed at the spoor. It was fresh, making her pull back instinctively in fear. Rivo whined and his fur lifted. The lion had passed by less than half a day ago, perhaps while they were climbing up to the pass. The depth of the print told them something of the size of the animal. Otak made with his hands the sign that meant "a big one." Maroo nodded.

The snow began to fall more heavily, and the lion's prints were obliterated before their eyes. They went back to their building and, in spite of tiredness, finished the snow house quickly. While Otak smoothed off the entrance tunnel, Maroo took kindling from her pack and scraped out the embers of the fire from the horn. The embers were hot, but there was no red glow. She blew gently, as she had seen Old Mother do. The red came, but died away before it could ignite the dry wood.

She blew again, feeding the sleeping fire with slivers of wood to tempt it into life. In her pack she carried a bow-drill for making new fire, but this was Old Mother's fire, and she wanted to have Old Mother's fire in her own hearth. At last she was rewarded. The wood smoked, then sprang to life. Soon the fire was roaring red, and the snow house grew hot. The children were too tired even to eat. They curled up in their furs with Rivo between them and slept till far into the morning.

When Maroo woke and crawled down the entrance tunnel, she knew from the silence that it was still snowing. Outside, snowflakes were flying thickly past; a deep drift was piled up against the side of the snow house, and the sky was heavy. There could be no possibility of leaving the snow house until it stopped: rocks and crevasses would be hidden, and they would never find their way safely across the top of the mountain. Nor could they hope to hunt, though the meat was running low, and so was time. Maroo counted on her fingers: the thumb and forefinger brought them to this shelter, and today would be the second finger. She crawled back inside to tell Otak.

For the rest of that day they sat in the snow house and waited for the blizzard to pass. Otak was restless and longed to go out and hunt. Maroo became increasingly stiff; every limb ached, and she realized that this was the result of her fall on the glacier. She found that she was covered with blackening bruises.

Otak took from his pack the horns of the ibex Areg had killed, and wedged them into the snow behind his sleeping place.

Maroo said, "Why did you bring those? They must be heavy."

"I wanted to," said Otak. "I shall always take them, everywhere I go." His lower lip wobbled, and Maroo said no more.

Strange noises penetrated the snow house: wind spirits moaned in the entrance tunnel and the smoke hole. They both remembered Old Mother's words about the mountain, how it was dangerous and they should cross it quickly "before it feels that you are there." And now they were trapped here by the blizzard, and surely the mountain spirits must know it. Already they had tried to drag Maroo under the ice.

As the day went on, the children became more and more uneasy. Once, when Otak went out to urinate, he came back wide-eyed with fright and reported seeing a spirit, a dark slinking shape, on top of the ridge above the snow house. While Maroo tried to reassure him, a terrifying scream came from nearby, followed by scuffling and snarling and a catlike growl. She and Otak clung to each other. Rivo barked and barked.

Maroo remembered the cat spirit that had haunted the echoing rock—and the disastrous ibex hunt that had happened there. But as they crouched together, quivering with fear, she also remembered Old Mother's advice about stories.

"Don't cry," she said to Otak. "I'll tell you a story." And she gave them each, including Rivo, a portion of the deer meat and began the story of the hare who challenged the sun to a race.

A day later Maroo's fund of songs and stories was running low and the meat was almost gone. Rivo growled and fretted in the passage, and Otak was whimpering with hunger and boredom. He wanted to go out and hunt.

"It's too dangerous," Maroo said patiently, yet again. "You might fall, as I did, or get lost."

"I could get a lemming, or a hare. I'm not afraid of the snow."

Maroo laughed contemptuously. "Yesterday you were frightened of the wind in the tunnel."

"So were you!"

"If I was, I didn't show it. *I* didn't start crying and asking for Mother."

Otak's eyes were red. "I hate you," he said.

Maroo was sorry, but did not know how to say so.

The blizzard was dying down, and she hoped that by tomorrow they could leave the snow house. She thought of that other snow house, two days' walk away on the Great Plain. If only they were all together! She imagined them sitting around her own hearth: Vorka, Tikek, the baby and little Nimai, Old Mother — and

Areg. She thought longingly of her father, missing his cheerful confidence. If Areg were here, they would not have quarreled; he would have made them laugh. Tears came quickly, and she turned aside so that Otak would not see. He might start crying again too, and then their pretense of courage would be over.

She crawled down the entrance tunnel, partly to hide her tears and partly to check the weather. The sky was darkening; the wind had dropped and only a few flakes of snow still fell. She came back, cheered.

"It's stopping," she said. "Let's go to sleep now, and be ready to move out at dawn."

She fetched clean snow from outside, put it in the bone bowl, and melted it with hot stones from the fire, sprinkling it with a handful of herbs from the pouch hanging from her belt. She handed the drink to Otak, feeling that she had done what Old Mother would have done.

When they had drunk, they curled up together and tried to sleep. But Maroo lay awake for a long time, thinking of the way ahead and the Pass of the Spirits.

═14═
Across the Pass

THE NEXT MORNING the blizzard had blown itself out. When Maroo crawled out of the entrance tunnel, she saw the snow piled into deep, smooth, glittering drifts. The sun was bright and the snow glare dazzling. Maroo knew that this was a day when a traveler could go snow-blind, but she was determined that they should move.

Rivo squirmed out of the tunnel behind her, followed by Otak. The dog charged into the smooth hollow in front of the snow house and rolled over and over. He stood up and shook himself, spraying the children with water. Otak laughed and threw a bone, which sank into the snowdrift beyond. Rivo plunged into the drift to retrieve it.

Otak clapped his hands. "He'll make a good hunter's dog."

Maroo nodded. Then, "What has he seen?" she asked.

Rivo had stiffened, staring at the untouched snow a sling-shot away. They moved closer to him. Otak whispered, "Look!"

There were tracks in the snow: the long, narrow tracks of a hare, moving in a curving line toward a low mound. Otak signaled to Maroo that the tracks were fresh; the animal had passed by only moments before. Both children were silent, for they knew that the hare might be hiding behind the mound. They stood still, Maroo with her hand on Rivo's collar. Otak crouched, his spear held ready to throw.

There was a movement, white on white, from behind the mound. Otak leaped and threw as the hare shot out. Maroo let Rivo go. The spear missed, and sank softly into the snow. Rivo bounded after the hare, but the hare was faster. It sprang away uphill, zigzagging in a series of wild leaps, leaving the dog confused.

Maroo watched until the hare merged with the bluish snow and it hurt her eyes to look. Otak had retrieved his spear. His face was dark. Maroo tried to cheer him by quoting a proverb of Old Mother's about a thousand false throws being father to the perfect throw — but Otak was not to be comforted.

Maroo sighed. "Come," she said, taking his arm. "You have all day to try again."

They rolled up their bedding and hoisted the bundles onto their backs. Maroo took hot embers from the fire and put them in the horn before stamping on the remains of the fire. They both pulled their hoods down low over their foreheads so that the fur fringe would help shade their eyes from the brilliant light.

The Pass of the Spirits shimmered far ahead, a snow-bright shape against the intensely blue sky. They could not bear to look at it; the air was full of sparkling particles of light.

They caught nothing to eat. Several times Rivo sniffed eagerly, pounced, scuffled, and came up with a vole, which he swallowed. Once they saw a flock of white ptarmigan burrowing for food in a snowdrift, but this time when Otak hurled a stone with his sling he was unlucky, and the whole flock rose crack-crackling into the air.

Otak cried with hunger and humiliation. "The mountain hates us," he said. "It won't let me catch food."

They walked all day until the sun hung low, and merciful blue shadows softened the gleaming landscape.

The shining icecap of the high pass was nearer now; they could reach it before nightfall. The softer light was a relief to their eyes. They noticed tracks of birds and small animals in the snow, and a larger track coming from behind a rock just ahead of them and going up toward the Pass of the Spirits. When they reached the track, they recognized the prints of the cave lion. The spoor was new.

Cautiously Maroo raised her head and looked up toward the pass. Nothing moved, but the way was littered with rocks and hollows.

"It was the same lion," Otak whispered.

Maroo agreed.

They stopped briefly, and she shared out the last of the meat. "We must get more meat," she said.

Otak flushed, thinking of the hare and the ptarmigan. "Rivo and I will hunt tomorrow," he said.

After a little while the lion's prints turned aside from the trail they were following and climbed up steeply toward some higher ground where jagged rock teeth broke through the snow. They stared up, but saw no sign of the lion.

The sun disappeared behind the high peak. The air grew cold and the wind strengthened. The Pass of the Spirits was now much nearer. They saw the way they would have to go, between a steep drop on one side and a towering wall of rock, almost the highest point of the ridge, on the other. A dark cave gaped in the rock like an open mouth, the cave Old Mother had told them about.

"Is that where the spirits live?" Otak whispered.

"I don't know." Maroo tried to sound indifferent, but she was desperately afraid of that black open mouth.

Otak chattered to hide his fear. "Perhaps it's the lion's cave. Is the lion a spirit?"

"I don't *know*," Maroo repeated irritably.

She was hungry and afraid and did not want to talk. The great outcrop of rock cast the mountainside into deep shadow, and they shivered with cold and fear.

Rivo seemed to sense the atmosphere of the place; he whined and clung close to Otak's legs.

All the time as they climbed up the increasingly narrow path, Otak and Maroo were glancing around warily for the lion. Maroo seemed to feel it behind her back, crouched on a high rock, ready to spring, but when she turned around there was never anything there.

They were approaching the pass itself, the narrow rock path between the steep drop and the cave.

The cave was vast. More than ever Maroo felt that it was the great black mouth of the mountain itself threatening to swallow her up.

It was dark in the pass, and their footsteps echoed. Rivo's fur stood on end and Otak had to jerk the lead to make him go forward. The cave gaped directly above them now. Its floor was level with their shoulders, and they could see in the entrance a scattering of bones, bat droppings, and tumbled stones.

The depths of the cave were in darkness, but out of them rose a smell that made Rivo whine plaintively and Maroo feel suffocated with fear. It was a musty odor of bats and owls, and the piled feathers, droppings, and bones of countless generations of animals. Overlaying all this was the powerful scent of lion.

Both children stopped when the smell reached them, paralyzed by fear as if the lion were there, in the cave mouth, watching them. At any moment Maroo expected to hear its deep-throated roar—from behind, from above, from deep in the cave. Where *was* the lion?

Her mouth felt dry, and she found she could not speak. She seized Otak's arm and urged him forward. Rivo pulled back on his lead. Maroo took the lead from Otak and walked on, dragging the unwilling dog. They walked as fast as they dared on the narrow path, all the time glancing up at the cave where the lion might suddenly appear and trying not to breathe the panic-making smell.

At last the cave mouth was behind them. The air smelled sweet again. The path grew wider and opened out onto a broad hillside. It was not yet dark. Maroo felt her fear ebbing away. She leaned against a rock and took off her pack.

Otak said, "This is almost the top of the world."

They turned all around. Below them in every direction were snow-covered mountaintops broken by gray rock. To the north the spine of the mountain range could be seen winding away; to the west, far down on the plain, lit by the sun's last rays, the Great River flowed in a series of shining lakes. The crossing place and the autumn camp were hidden by the mountain, but beyond it they could see the earth alive with a rippling movement of deer.

Old Mother had said that from this point the way was downhill and less dangerous than the ascent.

"We can be down and reach the camp by dusk tomorrow, maybe sooner," Maroo said. She counted on

her fingers. They would reach the family in time —
just in time, if all went well.

As if in warning, a snowflake landed on her cheek
and melted. The sky looked heavy. "Don't let there
be more snow," she prayed.

"I'm hungry," Otak said.

Maroo became aware of the gnawing pain in her
own stomach now that fear had subsided. "We'll hunt
tomorrow," she said. "We must make camp now. It is
going to snow. We'll go down there, in that tiny cave
between the rocks."

It was not a true cave, but a shelter created by leaning piles of rock. They squeezed in. The space stank
of fox, but they did not care.

Fire was needed. Maroo saw some bushes in a sheltered place lower down the hillside. "You go and fetch
firewood," she said. "I'll unpack the furs."

Otak put down his bundle, propped his spear against
the rock, and went off. Maroo untied the bundles and
began laying the furs inside the shelter. Out of the
corner of her eye she saw a movement. She swung
around, her heart leaping.

But it was not the lion. It was a hare, looking at her
with bulging wild eyes and gathering its muscles to
spring.

The three moved together: Rivo, the hare, and
Maroo, who seized Otak's spear and hurled it at the
leaping hare.

The spear hummed and struck. Maroo could scarcely

believe it. Rivo rushed to retrieve the hare, which was kicking feebly. Maroo ran after him and picked up the spear. She had never killed with a spear before. And the hare, which had magically appeared so near — surely the mountain spirits must have sent it?

They went back to the shelter, Rivo with the hare dangling from his mouth and Maroo with the blood-stained spear. Otak stood there staring, the bundle of sticks at his feet.

Maroo exclaimed, "Otak! We have meat! The spirits sent a hare!"

"You took my spear!" Otak said, tears of fury springing to his eyes.

"I had to. The hare appeared —"

"You took my spear!" Otak shouted. He punched Maroo, and the tears spilled over and streamed down his face.

Maroo's delight in the kill collapsed. She understood now, and tried hopelessly to reassure him. "You could have caught it, if you had been there. Anyone could. Don't you see? It was a spirit. It doesn't matter that I killed it."

"It does matter," Otak said, red-eyed. "You had no right to take my spear. And Rivo is my dog."

"He's ours!"

"He's mine for hunting. Because I shall be a hunter, not you."

"I'm sorry. But you were hungry and now we have meat. Let's light the fire and cook it."

"You light the fire," said Otak. "Girls make fire; they don't hunt." He kicked the dead hare. "This won't be much between us."

"You can hunt again tomorrow."

"I will," said Otak sulkily as Maroo fed the fire with twigs, "and I won't be sent off to fetch firewood. I won't leave you my spear again."

Maroo's patience snapped. "You're just a baby!" she said. "You can't catch anything yourself, and now you are angry because I can!"

As soon as she saw the hurt look in Otak's eyes, she wished she had not said it. When the hare was cooked, she tried to make up for her words, giving Otak most of the meat and saying she was sure he would catch something tomorrow.

The snow was falling steadily as they gnawed the last of the meat from the bones. They retreated promptly into their little cave, but it was too cold to sleep. They took turns sitting with their feet under the other's fur jacket, thawing their toes painfully back to life. Later they lay down, curled in the furs, and Maroo fell asleep in spite of the cold.

When she woke she saw snowflakes flying past the entrance to the shelter. She turned to Otak to tell him, but his place was empty.

With a cold feeling at her heart, she crawled to the entrance and squinted out into the thick-falling snow. Nothing. Both Otak and Rivo had gone.

=15=
The Mountain Spirit

MAROO WAS BREATHING FAST as she tied on her boots and pulled her jacket over her head. She tried to calm herself with the thought that Otak was just outside, surveying the morning. But she knew in her heart that it was not so. Rivo was gone. Otak's spear and sling were gone.

"You can hunt tomorrow," she had said. But when Otak woke this morning he must have known that she would not let him go out in a snowstorm, so he had crept out quietly before she woke. Where was he now? How could she find him?

She ran out into the storm. An angry wind shook and bit her. Shoulders hunched, the fur-edged hood pulled close around her face, she glanced quickly about, her eyes screwed up and watering from the cold wind.

No footprints. The snow would have covered them. No sound, either, except for the tearing of the wind. Perhaps Otak was on the lookout point above.

As Maroo climbed up the steep hillside, the wind

leaped down from the mountaintop and clawed at her clothes, driving sleet into her frozen face. She held her hood tightly under her chin with one hand and scuttled, head down, from rock to rock until she reached the place where they had stopped and rested yesterday.

The long vistas of mountain and plain were no longer visible; now there was nothing to be seen except a wall of driving snow. She searched for footprints but found none. She cupped her hands around her mouth and called, "Otak! Otak!" but the wind snatched her voice away.

"I must go back to the shelter," she thought. Surely, if Otak and Rivo had gone hunting, that was where they would come to find her.

She climbed back down toward the shelter, hoping all the time that Otak would be there when she arrived. There were footprints in the snow outside, but they were her own. The shelter was empty.

She went in and began to blow on the embers of the fire and feed it with twigs until it was blazing. She pushed the cooking stones into the base; Otak would need a hot drink when he returned.

Now there was nothing more to do, so she squatted by the fire and waited.

How long she crouched there she did not know. There was no sun to mark the shape of the day and nothing to break the monotony of wind and snow. She watched the endless snowflakes flying past, and it seemed as if she would be there for ever and the snow would never stop. Twice she got up, went out, looked around and called, but nothing moved or answered.

She squatted down again and began to think of the family in the snow house. She counted the days on her fingers; if she and Otak did not leave today, it might be too late to save them. She jumped up and began to pace around the tiny shelter. What should she do? Where had he gone? Would Rivo find his way back even if Otak could not?

Anger at Otak boiled up, mixed with guilt because she knew that it was her fault that he had felt driven to prove that he could hunt. He would not return now until he had caught something; she was sure of that. But to go out in such a storm! How could he ever find his way back?

She remembered Old Mother's warning: there must be no risks taken; if one of them was lost or injured, the other must go on. One must survive.

She had kept those words at the back of her mind, never thinking that she would need to make such a decision. But now — had the time come? She knew, with unwilling certainty, that Old Mother would not flinch from her duty if the food in the snow house ran low and rescue was not in sight. She would go far out on the plain and wait for death.

"I must go on without him."

The thought lay like a stone amid the confusion of anger, guilt, and anxiety in her mind.

She went outside and looked up at the sky. How late

was the day? She could not tell. Perhaps it was already nearing dusk. She knew that she could get down the mountain in less than a day, but in a blizzard like this she could lose her way and take much longer. Yet it had to be done.

"I'll call him once more," she decided.

She climbed up to the lookout and called his name over and over again into the howling wind. But no answer came.

She found herself crying. Perhaps he was already dead. Perhaps he had been dead before she woke up this morning. Or he might be injured, or trapped in a snowdrift, and waiting for help. She remembered her own terror when the glacier had tried to kill her, and how Otak had struggled to pull her out.

She climbed all around the hillside, calling and searching. She even went back on their tracks until she could see dimly through the snow the shape of the Pass of the Spirits. But surely he would not go up there?

She came down again, and at last returned to the shelter. The fire was low. She knew it was time to leave.

She abandoned Otak's fur bedding; it was heavy, and she still had a faint hope that he might return and need it. Among the furs she found the horns of the ibex that Areg had killed. She set them up to make an arch, as Otak had done, and prayed to Areg's spirit, "Keep Otak safe." Then she scooped the embers of the fire into her horn, slung her bedding roll on her back, and took up her staff, turning to what she knew must be the west.

The snow beat mercilessly in her face. The wind shrieked among the high rocks. She walked on, moving steadily downhill, prodding with her staff to test the ground ahead of her for dangers hidden under the snow.

She thought constantly about Otak and where he might be and whether he could survive. Once or twice the lion came into her thoughts, but the vision of Otak and the lion both roaming the mountain was too frightening; she shut it away. Better to concentrate on reaching the camp.

In spite of the blinding snow she tried to note features in the landscape: the shapes of rocks, the slope of the land, stunted tops of juniper just showing above the snow. Reaching a sheltered place behind a rock, she scrabbled in the snow and found three withered berries and some plants with long white roots, which she dug up and crammed into her mouth. The inadequate food made her more aware of her hunger, but she found nothing else to eat.

She saw, with alarm, that the air was darkening. It was almost dusk, and she was still high on the mountain. She must have waited most of the day for Otak.

"I won't stop," she decided. The blizzard made it impossible to see; the night could be no worse, she thought, though the idea of spirits nudged at her mind.

She went on. The day closed rapidly into evening, and still the snow fell. The rocks became vague and shadowy. She was tired, and trudged head down.

Suddenly, with a cry of disbelief, she stopped. She was back at the rock where she had dug up the roots! She must have walked ever since then in a great circle. Two sets of her own prints along the track confirmed it. She was lost. Shaking with fear, she darted about, frantically searching for the way. Everywhere looked the same. Panic seized her. She began to run, faster and faster, away from the rock, anywhere so long as it was away from that rock. She ran until her chest was burning, and still she could not stop. Her breath was coming in big tearing sobs. She dropped her staff and flailed at the air as she ran.

Run! run! run! her fear told her. But at the back of her mind she heard something else: Old Mother's voice warning of the dangers of panic. A man lost in the wilderness, she had said, could go mad and run blindly until he died of exhaustion. "If you are lost and the madness grips you, stop. Drop in your tracks, let your fear go, and the Earth Spirit will show you the way."

Maroo stopped, and stood panting. She fell to her knees and crouched on all fours with her head hanging. Slowly the panic subsided and she breathed more easily, but she stayed there a long time until all fear had gone.

When she got up, the sky was black and full of falling snow. She could not see, and yet she knew instinctively that she was facing west. She also had a sense of altitude and knew that she was about halfway down the mountain. She began walking calmly into the dark, snow-laden night.

She walked more slowly now, letting her body lead her. Besides, she was becoming tired, the way was dark, and she had lost her staff. The panic did not return, but her confidence ebbed with tiredness and the thought of Otak, deserted on the mountain.

She could not stop worrying about her brother and wondering if she had been right to leave him. He might have been so near when she was calling, but unable to hear her. The thought made her cry again, and the icy wind froze the tears on her face.

As she brushed them away she became aware that the snowflakes had been getting smaller for some time, and now — was the blizzard almost over? The wind was strong, but there was less snow.

She wondered if Otak would find his own way down the mountain. There were no stars to point the way. If only Irimgadu were shining! She longed for a sight of Old Mother's name-star; it would guide her, as Old Mother did.

As if in answer to her wish, the wind-blown clouds parted briefly to reveal flickering faraway stars. Wisps of cloud blew across them, eclipsing the light, then revealing it again. But Irimgadu remained hidden.

The blizzard was almost over. Maroo paused in relief and became aware of her aching body and stinging face. After the hours of snow-battering, she was exhausted.

"I won't sleep," she thought, "but I'll stop and rest."

She slumped under a rock in the lee of the wind, letting the tiredness drain out of her. In spite of her determination she must have slept. She jerked awake in sudden fright to find that the moon was shining on her face.

The moon was full and hung low in a black sky thick with stars. Irimgadu shone brightly. The wind spirits were quiet, no longer howling among the high rocks. Maroo's fear disappeared. Old Mother always said that the moon was friend to women and girls; it had woken her and made the mountain visible for her journey.

She got up. The mountainside was shining with a bright silvery light; rocks and bushes stood out, black-shadowed; the snow glittered. Maroo scooped up some of the sparkling stuff in her hands and sucked it. The cold hurt her teeth, but she was too thirsty to mind.

She lifted her bundle and heaved it onto her back. The mountain, a black, immense presence, reared behind her. She could not see the plain from here but sensed that she was now on the lower slopes of the mountain.

She turned confidently toward the west — and stood still in utter terror.

There on the path ahead of her, outlined in silver, and with every hair, every whisker, glittering, was the lion. Its eyes shone with silver fire. Its tail swished.

Maroo knew for certain that this was the mountain spirit. The silvery lion was the mountain itself, come to bar her way, challenging her for being so bold as to think she could trespass on it.

She stared into the gleaming eyes, willing them to let her pass. The lion did not move, but a low growl came from deep in its throat.

Maroo glanced quickly about. High rocks surrounded her. The narrow path was blocked by the lion. Slowly, without taking her eyes from the lion's, she reached behind her and felt inside her pack until her hand closed on something hard. She withdrew it. It was a torch: a short stake, one end coated with pitch.

Her eyes still held the lion's eyes. The low growl increased. The lion's breath made a small cloud.

Cautiously she reached for the fire horn at her belt. The fire was alive. She blew on it and the flames brightened. The lion raised itself, tensing for a spring. Maroo gripped the torch.

Pitch and fire united. The torch blazed, crackling and spitting, a red intruder in the silver night.

The lion snarled and spat. It backed away. Maroo advanced, holding the torch in front of her. She bared her teeth at the lion, but her hands shook with fear.

The lion snarled angrily, its tail whipping from side to side. It made a run at Maroo. She stood her ground and thrust the torch toward its face. It snarled, tossing its head and showing long, wicked teeth.

Maroo came nearer. She thrust with the torch again. The lion's paw whipped out, and she leaped away. She knew that one swipe from those great curved claws would maim her so that she could never get up.

The lion, seeing her hesitation, came on with a spring.

Maroo, with a cry of terror, pushed the blazing torch into its face.

The lion howled in pain and rage. It bounded away down the path, then turned and growled again.

Maroo knew she must show no weakness now or the mountain would defeat her. She walked forward resolutely, the torch held out, her eyes fixed on the lion's eyes.

Slowly the lion backed away. It crawled backward on its belly until it reached a place where the path opened out onto rock-scattered mountainside. Then, with one bound, it was gone, vanishing among the high rocks.

Maroo felt her legs give way. She dropped to the ground, extinguishing the torch, and sobbed with relief. She had won. She had overcome the mountain spirit. An enormous tiredness threatened to overwhelm her, but she forced herself to get up and walk to the place where the lion had disappeared.

There were outcrops of rock all around, but she was not afraid that it might be hiding there. It was a spirit lion; she had defeated it, and it had gone back to the spirit world. She looked up at the moon and made a sign of thanks. Then she sat down with her back to a rock and fell asleep.

She woke to the sound of bird song. Opening her eyes, she saw the sun beginning to rise. She got up, and then, despite her weariness, shouted for joy. She had reached the foothills of the mountain, and there on the plain below were the huddled tents of her people.

As she walked down the mountain, more of the camp gradually came into view: the flint workshops, the smokerooms where the deer carcasses hung, the people moving between the tents. The camp was huge: a great concourse of shelters and the smoke of many hearths rising between them. There were people from four tribes there. All the people Maroo knew of in the whole world belonged to those hearths, and she felt a great rush of happiness at the sight of them.

After her lonely trek down the mountain, and the hardships of the long journey with the family, she wanted nothing more than to be in a familiar crowd of people. Everything filled her with love and relief: the smoke from the fires, the sounds of laugher and argument, the smell of cooking meat, the ringing of the ax-maker's hammer, a woman singing tunelessly as she scraped fat from a hide.

All Maroo's tiredness left her as she ran eagerly down the last few steps of the mountain and into the heart of the gathering.

═16═
At the Crossing Place

IT WAS NIGHT: a cold frosty night vivid with stars, Irimgadu the brightest among them. And in the light of her star sat Irimgadu herself, cross-legged on the ground, thin, but erect as ever, her hair coiled into its cone and pinned with its three bone pins. With her sat Nimai and Vorka, and Tikek with the baby in her arms, and Maroo.

All around the family, fires were burning and women were preparing a great feast to celebrate their homecoming. Already drums had begun to tap and children had put on their beads ready for the dancing. Whole deer carcasses were being roasted over the hearth fires and drinks were brewing in leather buckets.

The family sat in the place of honor by Keriatek's hearth-fire, but the loss of Otak took all the joy out of their homecoming. Tikek's tears ran as she cuddled the baby. Old Mother looked drawn, and Maroo guessed she must be asking herself whether she had been right to send the children on alone.

Maroo counted on all the fingers of one hand the days that had passed since she came down from the mountain. The young men had searched the lower slopes the day she returned but found no trace of Otak. They had wanted to go higher, but the elders forbade it. The mountain spirit had taken Otak, they said; one life was enough. Maroo knew that Otak probably could not survive so many days alone, yet she still kept hope alive — he had his weapons, and the dog, and perhaps the magic of the ibex horns. . . .

The day she had arrived in the camp several young men from each of the four tribes had set off at once to find the snow house on the plain, taking food, furs, and sledges. Maroo, too tired to walk, had been pulled on a sledge so that she could guide them to the place. The men had traveled at a hunter's trot and reached the snow house in two days. They had found the family hungry but all alive. As soon as they were fit to travel, they had been put on the sledges and the hunters had pulled them back along the trail.

Maroo, watching the two men jogging ahead as they pulled the laden sledge she sat on, had had a fleeting vision of a sledge pulled by a pack of dogs — tame dogs like Rivo. She had wanted, urgently, to share her vision with Otak, knowing he would be captivated by it too. Then she had remembered that Otak was dead; she would never share any ideas with him again.

The journey had taken four days, and when at last they came in sight of the camp, a great shout had gone up; people had come running to meet them, the drums had begun to beat, and Keriatek and Sovi had offered up thanks to the Earth Mother for their delivery.

Otak was not there, but his spirit shadowed the feasting. Maroo turned to Old Mother and asked yet again, "Did I do right to leave him? Should I have waited longer?"

"No, you did right," Old Mother comforted her. But still Maroo felt guilty.

The people crowded around. The women began to hand out meat, hot and dripping with fat. They held it in gloved hands. Maroo was glad to be back with her people — but the man from the Blue Lake tribe was there, with his dog that reminded her of Rivo, and at the thought of Rivo and Otak lying dead and frozen on the mountain, the tears splashed down her face and she could not eat.

The feast went on all night. Maroo was too hungry not to eat a little. There was dancing and singing. Vorka sang a song about Areg and how he had died. Maroo became aware that songs were being sung in her honor; she would always be remembered now throughout the four tribes as the girl who had crossed the White Mountain and survived.

Another sound mingled with the drumming and chanting: something familiar. She saw that the Blue Lake hunter's dog had stood up and was barking. It barked frantically at something in the darkness beyond the firelight. The hunter and another man got up and went to see what was wrong. No one else had noticed, but Maroo watched, intrigued by the dog's behavior.

The men returned with two dogs. The other dog was a wild-looking thing with ribs showing and a plaited cord around its neck.

Maroo's heart leaped. She sprang to her feet and shouted, "Rivo!"

The dog bounded across the open space and jumped up at her, paws on her shoulders, licking her face with his hot tongue.

"Rivo! Rivo!" sobbed Maroo, patting the rough fur. "Where is Otak?"

And then she saw him.

The circle of people had broken and Otak staggered into the firelight. There was a moment's hush, a drawing back, and Maroo felt the hair prickle on her head as the unspoken thought reached her: is it a spirit? Then the dog rushed forward, and Maroo broke free and ran and flung her arms around Otak.

Otak said faintly, "I'm cold." He sagged and fell to his knees. The people crowded around.

Later, they heard what had happened: how Otak, lost in the blizzard, had fallen and sprained his ankle. Unable to walk, he had sheltered in a small cave with only the dog to keep him warm, shouting occasionally for help and hoping that Maroo would find him.

"You should have sent Rivo for me," Maroo said.

"I did. He went off, but perhaps he didn't understand, or perhaps you had already gone. He didn't find you, but he came back with a lemming and we shared the meat. After that he went hunting most days and caught enough to keep us alive until I could walk again. Then he helped me find the way down to the camp. He's a good dog. I would have died without him."

Maroo saw that the old men, Keriatek and Sovi, were listening. She looked at them. The two men murmured together. "The dog will come with us to the winter caves," they decided.

Maroo and Otak exchanged a glance full of happiness. Otak fondled Rivo, burying his face in the rough fur to hide his tears.

The camp was breaking up. The Blue Lake people had gone; others were leaving. They would go to their home caves and meet again perhaps in the spring, perhaps not until the next autumn gathering, for the land was vast and men were few.

The tents were rolled up, the last fires stamped out, the tent poles and deer carcasses piled onto sledges. Birds flew by, flock after flock, heading south. The sky looked cold. Winter had come.

Immense herds of reindeer spread out across the white plain. Maroo and Otak walked with their people along the trail to the winter caves, and the dog trotted beside them.